Lush

Books by Sasha White

PURE SEX

THE COP

LUSH

Published by Kensington Publishing Corporation

Lush

SASHA WHITE

APHRODISIA

KENSINGTON BOOKS
http://www.kensingtonbooks.com

Aphrodisia Books are published by

Kensington Publishing Corp.
850 Third Avenue
New York, NY 10022

All Kensington Titles, Imprints, and Distributed Lines are available at special quantity discounts for bulk purchases for sales promotions, premiums, fund-raising, and educational or institutional use.

Special book excerpts or customized printings can also be created to fit specific needs. For details, write or phone the office of the Kensington special sales manager: Kensington Publishing Corp., 850 Third Avenue, New York, NY 10022, attn: Special Sales Department, Phone: 1-800-221-2647.

Aphrodisia and the A logo are trademarks of Kensington Publishing Corp.

ISBN-13: 978-0-7582-1548-2
ISBN-10: 0-7582-1548-7

First Trade Paperback Printing: April 2007

10 9 8 7 6 5 4 3 2 1

Printed in the United States of America

Acknowledgments

Thank you to my incredibly creative and artistic friend, Deanna Walker, for listening to me yammer on endlessly about my stories, and just for being you.

Thank you to my editor, John Scognamiglio, for your support and your belief in me.

And thank you to my guardian angel, Roberta Brown, for always watching over me.

This book is a work of fiction. Please remember to always practice safe sex in real life.

Contents

The Principles of Lust

Prologue

At first glance, it was rude. Yet, the longer Teal looked at it, the more details she noticed, the faster her pulse raced. The photograph shifted from rude to . . . raw, as she looked past the shadowed anus and the pouting pussy lips.

She noticed the strength of the hands caressing those curved hips. The water droplets scattered over taut skin of beautifully molded buttocks and firm thighs, as if recently washed, but not dried. The background was dark, the bodies anonymous. There was nothing else to the photo. Erotic in its simplicity, the only thing that mattered was the touch of those hands and the sensations created.

The visible wetness that covered the woman's swollen sex made it gleam lasciviously, and Teal almost wished it were her who was bent over, being caressed, being prepared masterfully for a night of erotic attention. She swallowed and squeezed her thighs together as the photograph evolved from raw to . . . luscious.

It was in that moment that the idea came to her. She'd been feeling a little lost and alone, like she didn't have a purpose. Her parents were happy in their corner of the world, and her brother had found a career he seemed to thrive in. Yet for her, jobs came and went, men came and went. Nothing was a challenge anymore.

She knew there was more to life than partying, and she *wanted* to have goals; she knew she could do anything if she put her mind to it. She'd just never had a clue what she'd wanted to do before. Other than be successful, be independent. But right then, when she looked at that photograph, a lightning bolt struck and she knew.

She could use her ambition and drive, her salacious mind, and her ability to think outside the box, and finally carve her own special niche in the world. A successful and unique place that would be all hers.

And it would be called . . . Lush.

1

With less than a week until Lush's opening day, Teal Jamison didn't have time to fuck around, especially with something as frustrating as some punk kids spray painting nasty messages on the front of her building. Pissed off and stressed out about all the piddly little things that kept screwing up her plans, she strode into her soon-to-be art gallery muttering to herself only to stop dead in her tracks.

Anger turned to desire, and excitement of a different sort flowed through her at the sight that greeted her—soft, faded denim stretched lovingly across perfect tight male glutes.

All thoughts of temperamental artists, inconsistent suppliers, and juvenile delinquents evaporated as she watched the man straighten from his bent-over position and enjoyed the sight of a worn leather tool belt framing his ass perfectly.

Now, that's a work of art.

"Lookin' good, Zach," Teal purred as she dropped her backpack on the reception desk and continued in his direction. An hour or two of uncomplicated no strings naked wrestling with him would certainly take the edge off her stress level.

The carpenter ran a loving hand over the custom-built mahogany shelf he'd just installed before turning to her. "Thanks, Teal, but I'm just helping bring your vision of the place together."

"Oh, I've no doubt the gallery will be beautiful, but I was referring to the view when I walked in." She winked at him and gave his impressive form an obvious once-over.

His eyes flared brightly at her brazen comment before they closed in a slow, lazy blink that made her knees weak. When he looked at her again, the heat was banked and his smile was unhurried. "Well, that's the point of the setup, right? That the view be good from every angle?"

Zachary Dillon had come highly recommended as the finish carpenter for her new art gallery, and she'd made it a point to be completely professional with him. But his work for her was almost done, and she was ready to be more than his boss.

Her eyes followed his movements as he pulled a cloth from his tool belt and wiped his hands. His rough, calloused, manly hands were large enough to hold her C-cup breasts and make her feel small. Her nipples pebbled in response to her thoughts and she lifted her gaze to his.

"I was talking about you, darlin'." She couldn't help it. Flirting had always been second nature to her; man or woman, it didn't matter, she flirted and charmed . . . and usually got whatever she wanted.

From the start, just being around Zach had made her blood heat and her pulse race, but she'd remained professional. Teal prided herself on always being a professional, no matter what job she was doing, but she was working for herself this time. Lush was her place. Her baby. And she didn't want anything getting in the way of Lush's success, even her own libido.

Waiting until his work for her was completely done would

be the smartest thing to do, but she'd had a shit day and her emotions were running high. Maybe letting herself go this once would be a good thing. One night of steamy lovin' and her hormones would calm down, and she could concentrate on work again.

Yes, that was exactly what she needed.

She touched his bare arm lightly and gave him the slow, sultry smile that always got her whatever, and whomever, she wanted. "You're looking good."

"Thank you." His voice was a bit deeper as he shifted his weight to his other foot, taking him just out of reach. A knowing smile lifted his lips as he reached for the sweatshirt laying on a nearby stool, then pulled it on over his ragged T-shirt.

"I can't do anything else until I pick up more varnish, so I'm done for the day. I'll see you bright and early Monday, Teal." He picked up an old wooden toolbox and waved to her with his other hand. "Have a good night."

Teal said good night and watched him saunter away.

What the hell had just happened? She'd come on to him. In fact, she couldn't have been more obvious if she'd stripped off her clothes, and said, "Let's wrestle naked." And he'd walked away!

Men never walked away from her.

Her cheeks heated and she chewed on her lower lip. There was a definite attraction between them. She knew the spark of lust when she saw it. By investing all of her savings into opening the very first completely erotic art gallery around, she was betting her future on knowing that look.

So why would a big, healthy, and attractive man walk away from a woman he desired?

A few of hours later, Teal was working in the back room, and the question was still on her mind.

"Maybe he's just shy," the perky brunette said from her perch on top of a packing crate.

"No, that's not it." Teal shook her head and pulled the lid off the smaller crate on the table in front of her. She thought about the way Zach moved, the way he ran his hands over whatever he was working on, and a shiver danced down her spine. "He's way too . . . confident to be shy. He's quiet for sure, but he gives off this impression of restrained strength. Very strong and sexy, and completely alpha."

It was just after 10 P.M. on Saturday night and she and Brina Jo were in the spacious back room of the gallery, unpacking the first shipment of items. Teal had spent the past two hours on the phone trying to line up a cleaning crew to come and wash the graffiti off her building, but since the next day was Sunday, nobody wanted the job. She'd lined up a crew for Monday, though.

She'd been enjoying her time alone in the back room. The first bit of quiet time she'd had in a while.

When the idea for an art gallery that specialized in erotic art had come to her, she'd run with it, and that meant the gallery was pretty much all she thought about. She lived and breathed whatever job she was working when she worked it, and Lush was the most important job she'd ever had. It was all hers. Besides, full speed ahead and complete stop were the only speeds she knew.

Unpacking inventory in the back room was a bit of both for her. She got to work fast and efficiently, and since she was alone, she could turn off her brain for a while and just enjoy. But her brain hadn't cooperated. Instead, she couldn't stop thinking about a certain well-built carpenter and fantasizing about ways to get him naked.

Until she'd heard someone rattling the locked door of the gallery.

Thinking she might catch the graffiti punks, she'd dashed through the empty gallery only to open the door and find nobody. Well, nobody with a spray can, anyway. What she did find was a flyer with the words: *"House of Sin. You are going to hell."* glued to her front door. Slightly creeped-out, and tired of her own thoughts, she'd called her longtime friend and newly hired assistant, Brina Jo.

By the time Brina arrived at the gallery, Teal had scraped the flyer off the door with warm water and a putty knife and pushed it to the back of her mind. However, thoughts of Zach would not go away, so she'd blabbed uncontrollably to Brina about the brick wall hitting on him had been.

"If he's not shy, maybe he's not interested."

Teal snorted. "Oh, he's interested."

"How do you know?" Brina asked. "I mean, if he's as distant as you say and he's not gay, then how do you know he's interested?"

Turning away from the crate in front of her, Teal faced her friend. "I can *feel* it. Whenever we're in the same room together, the air fairly vibrates with pheromones, and it's not just me. I've caught him watching me, and I've seen *the look* in his eyes. He wants me, too." *Why wouldn't he?*

"What look have you seen in his eyes?" She glanced up from the clipboard she was using to catalogue the items Teal unpacked.

"The look of lust."

Brina Jo's eyebrows jumped. "Lust, huh? Are you sure it's lust and not just tolerance because he thinks you're crazy? He has been in and out of here for the past two weeks, he's seen your moods."

"Crazy is the way your husband looks at you!" Teal threw a handful of Styrofoam peanuts at her friend. "And my moods haven't been that bad. It's just a bit stressful getting this gallery ready to open in less than a month."

Brina cocked her head to the side. "Tell me again why someone with no experience in art whatsoever decided to open an art gallery?"

"I don't need to know art for this particular gallery. I know everything there is to know about desire, hidden and otherwise." Teal arched an eyebrow at her friend. "That includes what lust looks like, even in its subtlest form."

"If you're so sure of his attraction, why don't you just ask him out?"

Teal turned back to the crate in front of her so she didn't have to look at her friend. She hated to admit it, but even though Zach's "hard to get" act just made her want him more, she didn't want to ask him out first. It was silly, but it felt like, if she did that, she'd be giving him the upper hand. And that was something she didn't like.

She tried to think of a way to explain that to her friend as she reached into the crate and dug past the packing. She grasped the bronze sculpture within and lifted it out, scattering the little-styrofoam peanuts everywhere, and her jaw dropped. "Wow."

"You're not kidding." Brina Jo hopped off the table she'd been sitting on and stepped forward for a closer look. "That is . . ."

"Amazing," Teal finished for her.

"That's one way to put it. Are you really going to display it?"

Teal set the sculpture down on the table to her left. She wiped a dust cloth over it lovingly, taking in every detail. It was a couple making love. The female stretched out on her side with the male on his knees, straddling one of her legs while cradling the foot of the other against his shoulder. She was spread completely open. Her head was thrown back, her expression one of pure ecstasy. There was nothing hidden to the viewer as the man plunged his cock into her. His cock was as lovingly crafted as her sex.

Teal turned the sculpture around and found it beautiful from every angle. Every curve and crevice detailed to the point that her own sex clenched in anticipation of being filled.

"Teal?"

Brina's voice broke the spell that had fallen over Teal, and she pulled her hands away from the bronze couple. "Hmmm?"

"You're not really going to display that in the main room?"

Teal looked at her friend. "Of course, I am. Why wouldn't I?"

"It's very . . . it's so . . ." Brina Jo waved her hand about.

Teal watched her friend's cheeks flush as she searched for the right word. "Erotic?" Teal finally took pity on her.

Brina Jo planted her hands on her ample hips and rolled her eyes. "Yes, *erotic*. But blatantly so."

"Well, that's what Lush is for. I want it to showcase the erotic art that normal galleries think is too 'out there' or 'too edgy.' I can't call it an erotic art gallery, and then hide the most erotic pieces in the corner."

"True, but you know you're going to take some flack for it, right?"

Teal shrugged. "I'm prepared. Plus, I know that sex and sexuality is a huge part of human nature, even if some people like to pretend it isn't. I'm banking on a lot of people getting more turned on by these things than they thought possible." Teal smirked at her friend. "Just like you."

"Teal!"

"What?" She laughed. "You mean to tell me you're gonna go home to Doug after handling all these and *not* want to try out this position?"

Brina Jo's lovely chocolate eyes glittered and she bit her lip. "That's beside the point."

"No, Brina baby, that is *exactly* the point."

2

Zach desperately wanted to have one of the cold beers waiting patiently in his fridge when he got out of the shower, but he knew it would be a mistake. He was already on edge after being tempted by Teal's unspoken invitation, and alcohol would only weaken his control.

Instead, he toweled off and padded through his bedroom to the walk-in closet. He pulled on his favorite black leather pants, the ones that were worn and comfortable, already broken in. The ones that always put him in the right mind-set for a scene.

Bare-chested and barefoot, he went to the living room where he turned on the sound system that was wired throughout the house. The dulcet tones of the saxophone filled the room, and he settled into the comfortable lounge chair near the patio. Closing his eyes on the view of the Saskatchewan River as the sun set behind the skyline, he concentrated on his plan for the night.

Deep breaths in through the nose . . . out through the mouth. An image of the sexy and enticing Teal Jamison emerged behind his eyes and he ground his teeth together. No matter how seductive she was, she was too aggressive for him.

She had a palpable sexual aura that made him want to strip her down and tie her up so he could explore her to his heart's content. But as he'd worked in the gallery, he'd seen her assertive nature come more to the fore each day. While she was still immensely attractive, he knew they wouldn't fit.

To his way of thinking, aggressive women rarely had it in them to completely let go. To let him pamper, spoil, or play with them. They always wanted to fight for control of the relationship, in the bedroom and out of it. And while he enjoyed power exchanges, power struggles weren't his thing.

He breathed deeply again, focusing on the beating of his heart, slowing it to a heavy throb that settled in his groin as his body recognized the ritual. In his mind, he saw the room in his basement, a slim, soft female blindfolded and strapped to the lovingly crafted X-cross. He saw himself step closer, brace his hands on the cross, and lean in, dipping his head. The view switched and he saw the eagerly parted lips just beneath his, the same plump, luscious lips that had taunted him only hours ago at the gallery.

Zach's eyes jerked open and he cursed.

His heart was pounding, his cock was aching, and a small trickle of sweat ran from his temple. He shook his hands out, rolled his shoulders, and resettled himself deeper into his chair.

Forget about Teal, he chastised himself. *She's not for you.*

A short time later, the heavy chime of a doorbell sounded and Zach opened his eyes, ready to begin. With smooth movements, he got up and strode to the front door. He pulled it open and frowned at his curvaceous blond visitor.

"Hello, Jenna. I've been waiting for you, and you know how I feel about being kept waiting."

"I'm sorry, Master." Jenna cast her pretty blue eyes down

and clasped her hands together in front of her, waiting. "How can I make it up to you?"

A familiar hum of pleasure rolled over Zach as Jenna stepped into the room. He closed the door and turned to see her standing still and straight. Her body was tense and eyes glowing with an eagerness that tightened his groin.

"Let's go downstairs, shall we?" Zack held out his hand, gesturing for her to go first. She'd been to his home before, so Jenna knew which door led to the basement, his playroom.

She sashayed down the steps, her movements slow and deliberate, knowing that he enjoyed watching her move. Jenna was a dancer at one of the many downtown nightclubs. Both beautiful and intelligent, she teased and taunted men for money and used that money to pay her way through veterinary school. She didn't come to him for romance; she came to him because he gave her what she needed—relief from always being in control.

And they both enjoyed the way he did it.

She stopped at the bottom of the stairs and waited for him. He pointed to the sturdy wooden bench with the padded leather top that stood in the far corner, and she quickly made her way there. "Prepare yourself, Jenna," he said over his shoulder as he reached into the cabinet next to the bottom of the stairs.

After he'd retrieved the toy he wanted and inserted the batteries into it, he made his way over to her. She was naked by the time he reached her, having made quick work of her clothes.

"How do you want me, Master?"

"On your stomach."

She stretched out on the padded bench and he began to work. The sultry jazz music filled the silence as he ran his hands gently over her body from stem to stern. She expected a spanking for being late. It was a reasonable punishment that they could both find pleasure in as well, but one of the best ways to assert the top position, or power position, was to do the unexpected. So when she was trembling with anticipation, he bent her left leg at the knee and had her grip it in her left hand.

Then he bound it there with soft hemp rope.

He repeated the same thing with her right side and stepped back to admire the view. "What do you think, Jenna?" he asked.

Jenna turned her head and looked in the strategically placed mirror. Her cheeks flushed and she licked her lips. "Lovely, Master."

He had to agree. The picture of her curvaceous form, naked and restrained, was very appealing. But the look on her face, the flush in her cheeks, and the slight glaze to her eyes . . . that was what made the image truly lovely.

Zach reached for the vibrator he'd set on the nearby table and went to stand at the foot of the bench. "Keep your eyes on the mirror, Jenna."

From where he stood, he could see her pretty pink pussy, spread wide and wet. He tested her with his finger, closing his eyes and losing himself in the feel of her silky warmth. His mind started to drift with the music and his body responded. Hot blood flowed south, and his cock stiffened as he continued to tease her.

He inserted another finger and searched for the hard button of nerves with his thumb. Her cunt tightened around his fingers and she panted, her whimpers echoing through the room, blending with the music.

"Please, Master, let me come. Please." The husky voice went straight to his groin.

"Not yet," he murmured.

Zach pressed his hips against the bench, reveling in the slight pressure. He let go of the toy in his other hand, concentrating instead on the skin-to-skin sensation. With his eyes still closed, he reached out with his empty hand. He cupped her full bottom, squeezing it and running a finger teasingly down the crack there while he pumped into her faster with his other hand.

It wasn't enough. He removed his fingers and used his hands to press her thighs farther apart. Leaning forward, he opened his mouth and tasted her. Tart juices coated his tongue, and he proceeded to lick, suck, and eat at her until she was rocking wildly against him and crying out with pleasure.

When her cries subsided and her body shuddered gently under his hands, he pulled back and opened his eyes. He hadn't planned to eat her to orgasm. Hell, he hadn't planned to eat her at all. She'd been late, and the plan had been to tease her, keep her on the edge of orgasm without pushing her over until he was sure she couldn't take any more. But the scent of an excited woman had gotten to him. He'd closed his eyes, breathed it in, and couldn't help himself.

With a glance at Jenna's shining, satisfied face in the mirror, he suddenly knew why. When he'd closed his eyes, the image in his mind had been of Teal bound and naked on that padded bench.

Zach looked down at Jenna. With a suppressed sigh, he reached out, undid the hemp knots, and released her. He was still hard and throbbing behind the zipper of his pants, but he had no urge to take her.

He knew it then. He was really in trouble.

3

———————

Two days later, Teal bent over the large desk she'd set up in the corner of the gallery for reception and sales and watched Zach work. She wasn't getting anywhere with the freakin' inventory ledgers she was trying to organize because she kept getting distracted by his presence.

Something had changed over the weekend. Still calm and quiet, Zach's attitude had shifted subtly from distant and laid-back to watchful. She felt him even when she couldn't see him. Watching *her* in a way that made her blood thicken and pulse slow with a sensual heaviness.

Of course, being surrounded by erotic art constantly had made a low-level hum of arousal her constant companion. But whenever Zach was around, the level kicked up a few notches.

Her cell phone vibrated on her hip, dragging her attention away from the view he presented as he applied stain to a display podium and the sensations it aroused within her. She never should've hit on him, she thought as she unsnapped the phone from her waistband. He'd turned into a distraction she really didn't need.

She flipped her cell phone open without checking the caller ID. "Teal Jamison here," she said crisply.

"Wow, you almost sound professional," a deep voice full of humor came back at her.

"The phone company hasn't hooked up my freakin' phone lines yet so I've had to give out my cell number to all the business contacts." She spun on her heel to stare at the one rich burgundy wall in the gallery. She really did like the ivory and burgundy color scheme she'd chosen. She clapped a hand to her forehead. *Focus.*

"Dominick, I need a favor."

"Whatever you need, you know I'm there for you, sis."

If there was one thing in life she could always count on, it was her family. Her older brother was a well-known columnist for a local paper, and Dominick absolutely hated it when people tried to kiss up to him or use his name to get ahead. Teal didn't like to ask anyone for favors either, but her free-spirited hippie parents had made sure that no matter where they lived or what else was going on in their lives, they knew they could always turn to each other.

There was no such thing as a favor that couldn't be asked amongst family.

So she sucked it up and voiced her request. "I can't get anyone from the paper to commit to coming to the opening next week. I've got people from the indie art magazines, but I want—I need more attention to make Lush a success. I want someone from *The City* paper. Please . . . talk to Wanda Brooks for me?"

Teal had been told the society columnist didn't cover art gallery openings unless they featured a big-name artist or a charity. Since Teal was just starting out, she didn't have any big-name artists, and the only charity she could afford to donate to was her own. She'd sunk everything, and then some, into Lush.

Heavy silence greeted her request, and she rushed to fill it. "I tried to get them to listen to the unique angle of it being an erotic art gallery, but they wouldn't listen. I know if I can get some of the wealthier people of the city to attend, I'd have a good shot at helping create a big-name artist, as well as a successful gallery. You should see some of the stuff I've got here, Dom! Sculptures and photographs that are wickedly sensual and unique. People will pay the high prices for them, if only I can get them in the doors!"

"Awww, Teal." Her brother's voice was almost a groan. "I get what you need, but having me talk to Wanda's not a very good idea."

"Why not? Come on, Dom. She'll do it for you; women do anything you ask." Just like men usually do anything for her.

They'd been raised to believe nudity and sexuality were natural in all its forms, and that seemed to give them an air of openly sexual energy that they'd both learned to use to their advantage in life.

She peeked over her shoulder at the man working in the center of the room. *Usually* was the keyword there. The family charm didn't seem to be working on Zach.

"Wanda the Witch and I don't get along at all, Teal. Letting her know you're my little sister might bite you in the ass."

"Come on, Dom. Do this for me, please? You're a top dog at that newspaper, she'll listen to you." Teal hated the whiny note that entered her voice, especially since she was talking to her big brother, who sometimes liked to take his role as her protector too far. She'd worked long and hard to get him to understand that she could look after herself. But this was for business, not personal. He'd understand that. "I've never tried to cash in on your celebrity before, but I can't get any sort of response from her."

"Celebrity!" His derisive snort echoed clearly through the

21

phone lines. "I swear Mom carried a piece of the Blarney stone around in her pocket when she was pregnant with you, Teal."

"Please, Dom. Please, please, please." She injected as much emotion as she could into the last three words. It wasn't hard since she really did need the exposure.

"Damn it, Teal." A heavy sigh came across the line and her heart expanded. "While flattery will get you nowhere with me, blood will. I'll see what I can do."

Relief flowed over her. "Thank you, thank you, thank you, Dominick. I owe you."

"Yeah, you do. And you can repay me by telling me when you were going to inform me you're being harassed."

She squeezed her eyes shut. "I'm not being harassed, Dominick."

"So you haven't had a problem with graffiti and nasty messages?"

"There have been a few incidents, but it's just kids. The neighborhood."

"I don't like it, Teal. Tell me again why you think that warehouse is a good location for you?"

"Because it's close enough to Whyte Avenue that I'm easily accessible to tourists and shoppers, but far enough away that people won't feel on display when they walk into an *erotic* art gallery. I want them curious and comfortable, not embarrassed that someone might see them walking out with a paper bag in their hands." Nothing much about sex or sexuality embarrassed Teal, but she knew that a lot of people were like Brina Jo. People who kept all things sexual private and personal.

"Who told you about the pranks, anyway?" She hadn't mentioned it to *anyone*.

"I have friends who work in that area. They mentioned it. Speaking of which, they're going to stop by and check on things for you from time to time."

"Damn it, Dominick!" She took a deep breath. Temper was *not* the way to get through to her brother. "Just leave it alone. If I was having any problems, you'd know about them."

"Promise?" His voice was firm.

"I promise. Now, I have to get back to work. Go talk to Wanda Brooks for me."

They said their good-byes and she closed the phone with a snap. Damn it. The fact that others had noticed the crap that had been happening made her skin crawl. It meant she might not be imagining the malicious intent behind the messages.

4

Zach fought to steady his heartbeat as he watched Teal disappear into the back room. He hadn't been deliberately eavesdropping, but when he'd heard her plead so prettily, his cock had hardened instantly and his heart had started to pound. He'd figured her for a woman who would never plead, but maybe he was wrong.

And now, all he could think about was how he wanted to hear her plead for him like that.

Teal returned from the back room with a rolling cart full of framed prints. She stopped the cart nearby and picked the first one off the top and went about trying it on various spots along the far wall. He tried not to watch her, he really did, but his eyes just would not do what he wanted.

She looked damn good in her long, flowing skirt and classic white blouse. More sedate than what he'd seen her in before, yet still subtly sensual. Her dark hair was loose and free that afternoon, and when she stepped underneath the spotlight to hang a photo, the color came alive. It shone like polished mahogany, and his palms itched to touch.

His eyes followed the long line of her body as she stretched to place the frame properly, and he imagined her with her hands bound above her head, her body stretched out, awaiting his attention. He'd keep her hair down, so he could stroke it and play with it. He wondered if it was her natural color, or if her pubic curls would be different. Darker against her fair skin maybe.

She must've felt him watching her, because she looked over her shoulder in that moment and caught him staring.

Their eyes locked and the arousal tugged at his groin. There was definitely something about her that got his blood pumping. But he still hadn't decided what to do about it. When she looked back at what she was doing, he did the same.

He felt her approach and looked up at her from his squatting position. "Need a hand?"

"Actually," her lips tilted into a flirtatious smile, "I was just thinking of what I wanted for dinner tonight. There's a great Japanese restaurant down the road, would you like to join me for dinner when we're done here?"

Zach had to bite his tongue to keep from accepting her invitation as he straightened up. When he was at his full height, he looked down at her and shook his head slowly. "Thank you for the invitation, Teal, but I'm not sure that's such a good idea."

"Why not? You have about one more day's worth of work to do for me, then our business is done. I don't see why we should have to wait any longer to focus on pleasure instead."

"It's not that," he assured her. How could he explain his hesitancy to her when he wasn't even sure himself?

"Then?"

"I just don't think it's a good idea."

Her eyes widened and he took the moment of her surprise to move around the podium and get to work on the other side. He was almost done with it, and after that he had two more to do. Like she said, one more day of work; then his work for her was done.

If she let him, he could ignore the attraction for another day. It was for the best since he really didn't get the submissive vibe from her. He glanced back at her and met her puzzled gaze calmly. She nodded and gave him a weak smile before walking away, and he cursed the twinge of disappointment in his chest.

Neither of them spoke as they continued to work, but the tension grew in the silence. He'd just stepped back from the podium and was putting the lid back onto the can of stain when he felt her steady gaze on him. Ignoring it, he went back to where his tools were and gathered them up.

The abrupt click of her heels on the hardwood floor warned him of her determined approach.

"Okay, Zack, what's wrong with me?"

Schooling his expression, he turned to face her. "Who says there's something wrong with you?"

"You do. I know you're attracted to me. I can see it in your eyes. I can feel it tug deep inside my belly when you look at me." She scraped a well-manicured fingernail across his chest. "Yet, you won't even go to dinner with me?"

Honest amusement blended with the other sensations stirring inside him. She really was a force to be reckoned with. He pulled a cloth from his back pocket and wiped his hands while contemplating her.

"Do you always get what you want?"

Her head cocked to the side, she grinned at him cockily. "Pretty much, yes."

A chuckle escaped and he shook his head at her. "I think you're a very beautiful and sexy woman, Teal. I just think we wouldn't fit together well."

"Really? You've never seen me outside of this building, yet you can tell we wouldn't hit it off?" She licked those luscious lips suggestively and his cock twitched to life. "I think we'd fit together *very* well."

Zach pushed aside the mental image of their bodies fitting together perfectly and forced a light chuckle. "You really do go after what you want, don't you?"

"I do. And right now, I want you." She took a small step back and planted her hands on the curve of her hips. "But maybe I was wrong. Maybe you're just not man enough to handle me?"

She looked at him from under those long, dark lashes, the challenge in her eyes clear. His heart thumped and he mentally shook his head. Taking up the gauntlet she'd thrown down would be a real mistake. This woman was dangerous to more than his peace of mind. He knew it in his gut.

But he'd never been one to back down, so he opened his mouth and jumped in with both feet. "There's nothing wrong with you that some time in my basement wouldn't fix."

A delicate eyebrow lifted. "So you admit there's something wrong with me?"

"I wouldn't really say wrong. But I do think you're a bit too cocky. Yes."

Her eyes narrowed briefly, then she stepped forward again. Now she was close enough that the pointed nipples of her breasts brushed lightly against his chest and her breath heated his lips when she spoke. "It's not cocky when you can back it up. And I guarantee I can make you feel things no other woman ever has."

Hot blood roared south and his cock hardened fully behind his zipper. Damn, she was hot! He met her gaze and let her see the desire that was burning inside him.

"I don't doubt that a bit."

Wow!
The heat in Zach's gaze almost lit Teal's panties on fire. She'd

seen lust before, but it was nothing compared with what she saw in his gaze. Standing in front of him, breathing in his earthy scent, her sex moistened and throbbed, and her self-control flew right out the window.

"Is that a yes for dinner, then?" *Please be a yes.* If it wasn't a yes, she was afraid she might do something really rash. Something like strip her clothes off and ask him to fuck her then and there.

She held her breath as he stepped back and pulled a business card from his toolbox. He wrote something on the back of it with the pencil from his shirt pocket and handed it to her before picking up the toolbox. "I'm cooking; be there at eight."

Teal waited until the door swung shut behind him to fan herself with her hands. That man was more than confident, he was intense . . . and boy did he get her juices flowing!

5

It was five minutes to eight when Teal turned into the driveway of Zach's house. She double-checked the address on the back of the business card and looked back at the house in surprise. She didn't know what she had expected, but it wasn't the sprawling ranch-style house in front of her.

The house itself wasn't fancy or posh; it was quite simple, really. Elegant. The neighborhood was pretty high-scale, though, and with the placement of the house, she knew he had to have an amazing view of the river valley from the backyard.

Teal looked down at her cotton skirt and flowing tunic and cursed Brina Jo. When Teal had called her to ask for an opinion on what to wear to Zach's for dinner, Brina had suggested something casual, since it would be at his house. It seemed neither of them had thought that a carpenter would live in such style. Not that she'd expected a dump. The address would've given her a bit of a clue if she'd paid attention. And he *did* own his own business . . .

Teal gave herself a mental head slap. She knew better than to judge people on their looks or occupation. Her only excuse was that she'd been too focused on his body and the possibility of what was likely going to be dessert.

She also should've known better than to ask someone else what to wear. It was unusual for her to doubt her own taste in anything. But she was a bit unsure of herself where Zach was concerned. Shrugging her shoulders, she climbed out of her car and strode up the brick walkway that led to the door. None of the trappings mattered, it was the man himself and the fire he put in her belly that she was interested in.

And she was going to put that fire out tonight, once and for all, so she could get her mind back on business.

6

The doorbell chimed at three minutes to eight and pleasure flowed over Zach. She was on time.

He put down the knife he was using to chop vegetables and wiped his hands on the dishcloth as he strode to the door. When he opened it, his breath caught in his throat. Standing on his doorstep, smiling for him, she looked . . . right. Like she was right where she was supposed to be.

He was definitely in trouble.

He took a deep breath and tried his best to sound normal. "Come on in, Teal. You didn't have any trouble finding the place?"

They made small talk while she followed him to the kitchen. He already had a pitcher of cider on the table and he poured her a glass. "Make yourself comfortable. Dinner's almost ready."

He expected Teal to take a stroll around the main rooms of the house, at the very least, the patio. But she didn't. She seated herself at the center island in the kitchen, propped her elbows on the counter next to the waiting plates, and kept him company.

Despite the erotic tension that kept him on edge, their conversation flowed quite smoothly as he tossed the veggies into the skillet. Their talk of music shifted to movies, and he confessed he didn't even own a television; he was addicted to movie theaters. When she asked him where he learned to cook, he told her.

"My mother wasn't much for cooking, even when she was home. Cooking started out as a matter of survival for me, then grew into something I enjoyed. I even toyed with the idea of becoming a chef." He placed the grilled chicken breasts on the waiting plates.

The sautéed veggies were already on the plates and she was eyeing the food hungrily. "Really? So I'm in for a real treat tonight, then, eh?"

Desire flared deep inside at her words. He set aside the honey glaze he'd made for the grilled chicken and met her gaze head-on. "You have no idea."

The hunger in her eyes shifted and the air vibrated between them. Oh yeah, she was in for a treat, and for the first time in as long as he could remember, he wanted to skip all the niceties and give it to her immediately.

The woman threatened his much-valued control.

He watched her pink tongue dart out and slide across her bottom lip before she spoke in such a husky voice that he knew the tension was getting to her, too. "Why don't you tell me about it?"

Reining in his desire, he picked up the plates full of food and slid them into the oven to keep them warm. "I'd rather show you."

7

Teal looked around the basement in wonder. Zach had been full of surprises from the moment he greeted her at the door in threadbare jeans, a black button-up dress shirt, and bare feet, but his basement topped everything.

Standing at the bottom of the stairs, she felt his gaze on her as she took it all in. It was sectioned off, each corner having a different setup. The nearest corner had a chain hanging from the ceiling and a wall unit with various ropes and cuffs displayed. The next section had a huge wall-mounted mirror in front of a low wooden bench with a padded top. It almost looked like a gymnastics horse, but a bit wider.

Wide enough for a person's torso to blanket the top.

The next corner, the one to her immediate right, held a large, dark, wooden X-cross with padded restraints on all four points. The wood was polished to a high gleam that showed such pride and workmanship that she just knew Zach had built it himself. Then she noticed the matching armoire next to it and wondered what surprises it held.

When she turned to peek around the staircase into the last

corner, she saw no kinky bondage furniture, but two closed doors.

"What's in those rooms?"

"If you're good, you might find out."

Teal's head snapped around and she looked at him. She'd felt those words like a finger stroke between her thighs.

"If I'm good?" A lightbulb went on in her head and a surprise jolt of desire washed over her. "So that's what you meant when you said there was nothing wrong with me that some time in your basement wouldn't cure?"

His slow, lazy blink sent a shiver down her spine. Dinner was forgotten as her skin tightened everywhere and she imagined herself naked and strapped onto the X-cross. How delicious would his big, strong, workman's hands feel working her over?

The idea was appealing, more appealing than she'd ever imagined, but . . . "I admit I'm surprised. You don't strike me as the type of man who needs to dominate a woman to get pleasure."

His eyes flashed and his lips lifted at one corner in a half smile. "For me, it's not so much about domination as it is about being in control."

She shrugged. "Control, dominate, what's the difference?"

He led her over to the X-cross. "There's a big difference. I like to test the limits of my control, as well as a woman's. Giving her pleasure, watching her respond to stimulation, seeing the desire build inside her mind, in her body . . . It's an amazing thing. And even though I like to restrain my playmates, my dominating them is an illusion. They are ultimately the ones in charge of the situation."

She reached out and touched the padded leather cuff attached to the cross. "How is she in charge if she's tied up?"

"Trust." His eyes met hers and she saw the truth in them. "It all comes down to her trusting in me. Trusting I'll stop when she says to stop, or give her more when she begs. Trust in my control and my ability to give her the release she needs. Sensual, emotional, or physical release."

The world narrowed and all her attention focused on him and the excitement coiling low in her belly.

"Okay." She patted her hand against the polished wood of the cross. "I want to try this one."

Zach threw back his head and laughed. When he looked at her again there was something else mixed with the banked heat in his eyes. Something like . . . affection.

"How about we eat first?" he said with a smile.

Zack struggled to keep things light as he put the plates on the already set table and pulled a chair for Teal. She sat down, and unable *not* to touch her, he let his fingertips skim across her shoulder as he pushed her chair in. Heat zipped up his arms and spread though his body at the contact, and he kicked himself in the ass for inviting her over for dinner.

They should've gone out. If they were in public, she wouldn't know about his basement setup and she wouldn't have offered to get on the cross for him. An offer that bothered him.

Zach wanted to show her it was okay to let someone else be in control every now and then. He wanted her to experience the joys of letting go, to know that trusting someone wasn't a weakness. But her quick offer to submit made his radar hum. It had been her way of maintaining control, not giving it up.

"Wow." Her softly uttered exclamation brought him back to the present. "This is amazing! I can't believe I watched you prepare it, and it took you less than fifteen minutes!"

"I'm glad you like it. Often, I find that when it comes to the basic needs in life, the simpler things are, the better they are."

"You sound like my mother." They continued to eat and she

told him a bit about the way she was raised. He was a bit surprised to find out her parents were modern-day hippies. "They believe in natural foods, holistic healing, and free love."

"Free love?"

"That's not to say they screw around on each other, just that they could if they wanted to. They've never formally married, and Mom says that by restricting people's desires, they're restricting their souls, and she wouldn't dare to do that."

Interestingly enough, he understood what she meant. "And you? Do you believe that?"

"Yes, I do."

He nodded and they ate some more in silence. Zach knew then why he hadn't taken her up on her offer downstairs. It was because he'd come to like her. Not just be attracted to her, but to like her, the woman. His instincts had warned him she'd be trouble, that she was dangerous to him, and now he knew why. Because for once in his life, he looked at a woman and wanted more than a playmate.

He wanted a partner.

He wanted *her* for a partner!

Dumbstruck, he stared at her across the table. She was strong, smart, driven, and clearly a very sexual creature. He didn't want to just play, with her. He also didn't want her to *give* him her trust; she would never give something so valuable away. He had to earn it. . . . He wanted to earn it. Because if he earned it, there would never be any doubt about it—for either of them.

He sat back in his chair and just watched her. Contemplating his epiphany while enjoying her company. When she told him about taking business in college, but never mentioned art, another thought occurred to him. "You don't have an artistic background, do you?"

Teal hesitated, taking his measure before answering. "Nope, not at all."

"Is that why Lush is going to specialize in erotic works?"

"Exactly!" She beamed at him. "It's about more than art and more than sex. It's about the principles of lust."

"And those are?"

"Recognize it, then embrace it. People are too wrapped up in what's wrong or right, what they're taught is appropriate, and what is dirty or bad. I want to show the many different levels of eroticism there are, from subtle to explicit. And that it's okay to desire any and all of them. That these emotions are gifts to us that shouldn't be denied or restricted, but embraced."

The pleasure in her expression and passion in her words made his heart pound. There was so much more to her than he'd originally thought!

He waved a hand at her almost empty plate. "Are you finished?"

"Oh. Yes, I am." She looked down at her plate, as if she'd forgotten it was even there. When she looked back at him, her eyes sparkled wickedly. "So, what's for dessert?"

8

"You are."

When Zach stood up, pulled her chair back for her, and took her by the hand, she expected him to lead her to back to his basement. There was no doubt in her mind they'd end up naked that night, and she was pretty certain he had the same plan in mind, so when, instead of leading her downstairs he led her to the living room sofa, she was surprised.

He settled into the center of the long leather couch and gave her a steady stare. "Why don't you sit on my lap?" he asked, his husky voice stroking her insides. "And we can get started."

Blood heating and pulse pounding, she straddled him with her flowing skirt bunched up on her thighs. The soft denim of his jeans against her skin was a delightful contrast with the hard muscles of his legs. She hummed her pleasure and leaned forward to kiss him, only to have his hands tighten on her waist and hold her back.

Zach shook his head slowly and began to slide his hands over her ribs, then around and down her back. She watched him watch her as he slid his hands over her hips to her thighs.

One hand slipped under her skirt, and she gasped at the skin-on-skin contact.

His hand was rough and calloused, but his movements were gentle, and the heat from his touch spread quickly up her thigh to her pulsing sex.

"I think it's best if we take things slow, don't you?"

A pang of disappointment went through her. But she found herself nodding, almost as if the movement of his thumb rubbing lazily at the inside of her thigh was hypnotizing her. Calming her, yet arousing her at the same time.

"Kiss me, Teal."

Without a second thought, she leaned in and pressed her lips to his. The kiss started out gentle and seductive, lips rubbing together, breath mingling. She gripped his shoulders and slipped completely under his spell.

Their breathing got louder, replacing the Celtic music in her ears as tongues danced and teeth nipped. She slid one hand around his neck and up to cup the back of his head, her fingers delving into the softness of his thick hair as her other hand slid from his shoulder to his chest. Muscles twitched beneath the palm of her hand and she felt his heartbeat. It matched hers.

She shifted on his lap, trying to get closer to him. She wanted more . . . She *needed* more.

His fingers tightened on her thigh, but that was it. He didn't slide his hand higher or try to move things along. Impatience mixed with the arousal swarming her senses, and she tore her mouth from his, then gripped the hem of her shirt and tore it off all in one move.

When she leaned forward to kiss him again he pulled his head back slightly.

His hands gripped her hips, stilling her unconscious rocking. "Shhhh," he crooned. "Slowly. Let's learn about each other."

"You're hot and hard, I'm soft and wet. We'll fit together real well. What more is there to learn?"

"Remember what you said at dinner? Recognize lust, then embrace it . . . Try to do that for me, Teal."

She groaned and ran her hands restlessly over his shoulders. She leaned in and whispered in his ear as one hand started to undo the buttons on his shirt. "I'm trying, but you're going too slow."

His husky chuckle filled the room. He tangled one hand in her hair and pulled her head back gently to expose her throat. He scraped his teeth across her neck, sending a shudder rippling through her.

Her fingers made fast work of his buttons, and she finally got her hands inside his shirt and against his skin. She weaved her fingers into the light dusting of hairs there, searching for and finding his little male nipples.

They were already hard and she played with them, tweaking and rolling them between her fingers the way she wanted done to hers. His gasp of pleasure was music to her ears. "You're not embracing it, Teal, you're rushing it."

His lips found the sensitive spot behind her ear and his hands ran over her waist again, up across her ribs. His calloused palms scraping against her skin erotically, leaving a trail of fire wherever he touched. "Close your eyes, feel my touch. Feel it, and enjoy it for what it is . . . and trust that I'll please you. You don't need to rush it; I won't leave you hanging. I promise."

She tossed her head back, rocked her hips, and another moan slipped from her lips. God, she felt so good! It was more than just turned on. She was all warm liquid emotion. His touch calmed and set her on fire at the same time. She wasn't even aware that he'd removed her bra until his hands cupped her breasts, his thumbs rubbing back and forth over the aching peaks.

"Tell me, baby," he whispered as he scraped his teeth against her neck. "Ask for what you want."

She widened her thighs and rocked against the hardness behind his zipper. "You. I want you."

He pushed back against the sofa, putting a bit of space between them. "I'm yours."

Teal planted her lips against his, thrusting her tongue into his mouth and making quick work of his zipper. He lifted his hips, lifting them both off the sofa, and she shoved his jeans low enough to completely free him. When he settled back on the couch, she was already reaching for his cock.

Long and thick, he throbbed hotly in her hands. Her insides clenched and her pussy ached to be filled. His hot hands slipped under her skirt, palming her bare ass cheeks and teasing her senses until she panted the word "more" against his jaw as she nuzzled his neck.

His hands met at the thin elastic on her hip and, with a sharp jerk, snapped it. He did the same on the other side, pulling her skimpy thong away from her body. When he didn't immediately touch her, she sat back and saw that he'd lifted her panties to his face and was breathing in the scent, his eyes gleaming from above the delicate cream lace.

"Embrace it," he reminded her, and held the bundle up for her.

Meeting his gaze, she held his hand in hers, leaned forward, and inhaled the scent of her own sex. Musky and slightly spicy, it filled her head and fired her blood up even more.

"Good girl," he purred. His other hand reached between her thighs. His fingertips brushed across her swollen pussy lips, and her whole body jerked in response. She dropped his hand, gripped his shoulders, and braced herself up on her knees so he had better access.

"More. Inside me, please."

Zack guided her hips down while the head of his cock slipped inside, stretching her as he filled her slowly and surely.

"Yesss," she groaned. She immediately tried to rock on him, but his steady grip stopped her.

"Look at me, Teal." A hand cupped her jaw and he gazed straight into her eyes. Their gazes locked, and his hand trailed down her neck, over her collarbone, slowly, until he covered her breast. "Keep your eyes on me. I want to see every emotion. I want to see your pleasure, your joy as you come."

He cupped her breast, squeezing it and tweaking the rigid nipple as he began to move inside her. Small thrusts, not more than an inch in and out he went. The slow, teasing movements made every move, every stroke, every sensation that much stronger. When his thumb settled on her clit, the jolt of pure pleasure that zinged through her made her cry out. Yet their gazes remained locked. His dark eyes brightened in their intensity. She saw pleasure, confidence, pride, and worship there. Before she could grasp the concept of it all, he pinched her clit and her nipple at the same time and her world shattered.

She threw her head back; her cries echoed through the room mingling with his husky praise. "That's it, baby, come for me. Feel the pleasure, enjoy every second, every sensation."

When the explosions stopped and she settled against his chest, there was still an ache deep inside. She rocked against him some more, a small whimper escaping.

"Oh, you need it good, don't you, baby? That wasn't enough for you." His hands cupped her ass and he rolled. Suddenly, she was on her back on the sofa and he was seated firmly between her thighs. He braced himself on his elbows and looked down into her face with glowing eyes. "It wasn't enough for me either."

"Fuck me, Zach," she whispered. "Please."

"Oh, yeah." He pulled out and thrust home hard. No more slow and steady.

"Yes, yes," Teal panted. She braced one foot on the edge of the sofa and threw her other leg over the back of it, hooking her knee so she could tilt her hips up and take everything he gave her. She slid her hands around his ribs and raked her nails along his back as he pumped his hips and thrust deep and true each time.

It didn't take long. Her body tightened and her pussy clenched around his throbbing cock as it pulsed deep inside her, hot come filling her up. She curled her body up and bit into his shoulder to stifle the scream ripped from the center of her being as every muscle within her tightened and then released in exquisite pleasure.

9

He knew before he opened his eyes that she was gone.

Zack rolled over in the king-size bed and glanced at the clock on the nightstand. Four-thirty in the morning, and she'd snuck out.

Part of him couldn't blame her. The night before hadn't exactly gone as he'd planned either. Although why he expected it to follow his plan he didn't know. If he were able to follow any sort of a plan where Teal Jamison was concerned, she never would've been in his house, let alone his lap.

He'd known, from the moment he shook her hand on the day they met, that she was dangerous to his peace of mind. But he had to be cocky and think he could control his emotions as well as he could control his body.

It was simple really, he thought, as he lay sprawled out on his back staring at the ceiling.

After actually talking to her and getting to know her, he liked her. He surprised himself by liking her aggressive flirting and her "I dare you" attitude. It looked like he'd finally met his perfect match.

The big question now was . . . What was he going to do about it?

10

"Goddamn it!"

"What? What happened?" Brina Jo came running out of the back room, scissors in one hand and packing tape in the other.

Teal waved her hand in the air angrily, her temper in full swing. "I stubbed my toe on the corner of the fuckin' desk."

"That's it?" Brina glared at her. "Jesus, woman, you scared me to death yelling like that. What's wrong with you?"

"Everything. Nothing." Teal threw her purse on the reception desk and planted her hands on her hips. She glanced around the gallery real quick but didn't see Zach. They were alone. "Last night didn't go the way I'd have liked. Then this morning Dominick called to tell me how much I owed him for getting Wanda Brooks to make an appearance at the opening on Friday."

"Well, that should've put you in a *good* mood."

"It did. Until I got out of the shower and heard the voice message the caterer left. It seems they overbooked themselves and are backing out of the opening. So now I have no food, no drinks, and no servers!"

"Oh."

The women looked at each other. Brina knew about the flyers and the graffiti, and now this . . .

"I'm really starting to wonder if someone, or some *thing* is seriously working against me here." There was a slight tremble in her voice that had nothing to do with temper.

"Whoa! What is going on with you, Teal? You know little things like this always happen when they can do the most damage. It's why some people get what they want out of life and others don't. You taught me that, and there is no way I'm going to let you start thinking like a defeatist now!"

"Things are . . . it's just that . . . last night . . . Damn it!" She threw her hands up in the air.

"Breathe, Teal. Sit down and tell me what is going on." Brina steered Teal to the chair behind the desk, then sat on the edge of it, directly in front of her. "Start with last night. How did things go at Zach's?"

Teal lifted her left foot and placed it on the edge of the desk. While she examined her toe to make sure she hadn't broken it, she told her friend about Zach.

"I gotta tell ya, he shocked me in more ways than one."

"Well, it doesn't sound like anything bad, though. He has a nice house, is a good cook, and a bit of a kinky bastard." She grinned. "He sounds perfect for you."

Teal nodded slowly. "Yeah, except he actually didn't get kinky with me. When he showed me his toys in the basement, I thought we were going to get busy. Instead, when I said, 'Tie me up, baby,' he said, 'Let's go eat dinner now.'"

The rejection hurt much more than it should've.

Brina leaned back on her hands and eyed Teal. "Are you telling me you didn't have sex with him?"

"That's not what I said."

"Would you just spill it all?"

"After we ate dinner, we had a make-out session on his sofa that got a bit out of hand. Then he carried me to his bedroom and we had normal, straight-up, missionary sex."

Straight-up missionary sex that had still managed to blow her mind. When she woke up sprawled on top of the guy, thinking that his heartbeat beneath her ear was the sound she wanted to wake up to every morning, she knew it was time to run.

And run she had.

Brina was looking at her like she was crazy. "What's wrong with regular sex? There's a reason missionary is the most popular position, Miss I-know-everything-about-lust."

"Yeah?" Teal smirked at her. "And what is the reason?"

"It's the most intimate."

It hit her right between the eyes. That was why she was so freaked-out by Zach. Somehow, someway, he'd managed to control their whole night, without using any physical restraints, and it had been extremely intimate. She'd been so comfortable with him that she'd forgotten to keep her guard up.

Her shock must've shown on her face because, without another word, Brina Jo picked up the phone on the desk next to her and dialed. At least something was going right. The phones had obviously been hooked up.

"Hi, honey," Brina said into the phone while Teal just sat there trying not to think too hard. "Don't you have a cousin or something who works at a hotel restaurant downtown?"

Teal watched as Brina Jo hung up with her husband and then

dialed again. Fifteen minutes later, they had a new caterer that would provide full service for the opening. At a family discount, no less!

"Done." Brina waved the scissors in her hand at Teal and hopped off the desk. "Now, let's get to work. You have a gallery to open."

"Didn't your mother ever tell you not to run with scissors in your hand?" Teal teased as they made their way to the back room together. With only four more days until Lush opened, they needed to get the rest of the stock unpacked.

"I haven't listened to my mother since the day I met you. You're a bad influence, you know?"

The women continued to joke around, and soon Teal's heartbeat was normal again. Determined to stay on track, she did her best not to ask about the lack of Zach's presence. He still had one more podium to stain before he was done there. She'd sort of been prepared to see him when she walked into the gallery, and even though she hadn't said it to Brina Jo, his absence had been another of the things that had put her in a bad mood that morning.

The two women had worked out a good system for unpacking and cataloguing items, so they worked smoothly for a couple of hours. When lunchtime hit and Zach still hadn't come in, Teal started to worry.

"Did Zach come in this morning?"

Brina looked at her steadily. "Yes, he did, actually. He didn't stay long, though, and said he'd be back later this afternoon."

Relief and panic hit her at the same time. She didn't like the look in Brina's eyes, so she tried to change the conversation.

"Sushi for lunch?" she asked brightly as she brushed bits of Styrofoam from her blouse.

"It's okay, you know?"

"What's okay? Sushi?"

"It's okay that you like the guy. That you might want more than sex with him."

"Sushi it is," she said, and headed out to pick up lunch.

11

By four o'clock, Zach still hadn't called or made an appearance at the gallery. Teal didn't know what to think, and she was pissed off at herself for caring. After all, she'd really only wanted a good fuck from him, and she'd gotten it. That should be the end of story.

Should be.

Yet, somewhere, somehow, she'd developed a desire for more.

One of the benefits of having hippies for parents was that she knew herself very well. Both she and Dominick were taught to analyze their own emotions and responses right from the start. So she knew that her need to be commercially successful and to be her own boss came about as a form of rebellion against the laid-back lifestyle her parents still retained. And she knew that she was scared of the intensity of her feelings for Zach.

Especially scary was the urge to relax and let him take care of her.

The only time she'd ever let someone cook for her without

getting up and taking over was when she was in a restaurant. She liked being independent and self-sufficient. Too many years of being dependent on her parents' lackadaisical lifestyle had made her into a bit of a control freak. She knew that.

But when Zach had been cooking, there'd been such an air of pleasure about him that she knew he was doing it because he truly enjoyed it, so she'd relaxed and enjoyed it, too.

When he showed her his basement, he'd surprised her. But the shock wore off quickly, and she was surprisingly turned on by it. As much as the thought of giving up control scared her, the thought of giving it up to *him* intrigued her.

A sudden thought had her spinning on her heel and heading out into the gallery. There, on the far wall behind the reception desk, was the photo that had started her on this path.

The whole gallery was painted a very light cream shade. A classy, yet neutral color that blended well with the natural wood shelves and display podiums Zach had built for her. Everything was set up to show all the pieces equally.

Except the wall behind the reception desk.

It was painted a rich, deep burgundy that drew the eye.

Teal stepped closer and thought back to what had enthralled her so about that photograph. It was subtle, but it was there. Even when she'd used the word "masterful" in her mind before, it hadn't clicked. But the position of the woman, bent over and exposed . . . and the way the hands were both gentle and commanding . . .

The photo had aroused her, but it wasn't the explicit nature of it, or even the naughty details that had done it. It was the sense of complete openness.

The sense of complete trust.

Zach parked his truck in front of the gallery and sat there for a minute. It was almost six. He'd meant to be there long before then, but it had been one of those days. The good thing about the day being so busy was that he hadn't really had a chance to think about Teal and what he was going to do. Should he bring everything up and out into the open with conversation? Should he tell her that he thought he was falling for her? Or, should he just pretend that nothing had happened? That she hadn't knocked his world off its axis, and then snuck off without a word.

With a sigh, he got out of the truck just as Brina Jo was exiting the gallery. She saw him coming and waited.

"A bit late to start work, isn't it?" The smile she gave him was friendly but a bit reserved.

"Busy day lining up the next couple of jobs. This one *is* almost done."

She nodded. "Does that mean *you're* almost done here?"

Zach wasn't sure how to answer that. What was his next step? May as well be honest. "Done with the work? Yeah, I've only got a couple more hours and everything should be good to go. But I'd like to think that there's more for me here than the job."

Brina Jo's smile brightened. "A word of advice?"

He nodded.

"Don't give up, and don't give in. She's not as strong as she pretends to be." She patted him on the shoulder and walked away.

Figuring that for good advice, he pulled open the gallery door and went looking for trouble.

12

Zach found Teal in the back room, surrounded by unpacked crates and a variety of shimmering glass pieces. The one in her hands looked like glass dildo. A very *large* glass dildo. "Teal?"

She jumped and spun at him, dildo raised above her head like a weapon. When she saw him, her arm dropped and her other hand went to her chest. "Jesus, Zach! You startled me."

"Sorry." He gestured to the oversized phallic toy in her hand and chuckled. "I, uhmm, hope you don't plan on using that on me? In any way."

"What? No." She laughed and held it up for him to see. "With a price tag of almost a thousand dollars, it's a little out of my price range for a sex toy. Not that I'd want to use it on you. Or myself for that matter." By the time she was done talking, color had flooded her cheeks and her eyes darted about the room. She was looking anywhere but at him.

"You don't use sex toys?" Her almost shy behavior made it impossible for him not to tease her.

Her color deepened, but she rallied fast. "I admit to having a toy chest of my own at home, but it's nothing compared with yours."

His heart thumped at her sassy smile and quick recovery. Never mind that she'd just given him the perfect opening. "Did you like my collection?"

She put down the glass and leaned against the nearest crate, folding her arms across her chest. Everything about her body language said she was backing away, putting up walls between them. But when she lifted her head, she met his gaze head-on. "It was impressive, and pretty surprising."

"Impressive is good," he said as he walked closer to her. He didn't stop until he was close enough to see the dark flecks in her amber eyes. "Why so surprising?"

"I didn't peg you as the real kinky sort. Lusty for sure, just not kinky."

"I'm not kinky a hundred percent of the time. As you learned, I'm quite capable without all the toys, too." One more step and he placed his hands on the crate behind her, bracketing her hips.

He knew he was crowding her, but he didn't care. He'd gotten a good glimpse of something real and deep in her gaze, and he was going for it.

"Last night was a good time," she agreed.

Although her stance hadn't changed, Teal's eyes had darkened and her voice had taken on a breathy quality that made his dick throb. "Just a good time?"

"Okay, a very good time."

He watched as the tip of her little pink tongue darted out and dashed across her bottom lip. He leaned in until his lips were almost touching hers, and spoke softly, "I want more."

He heard the hitch in her breath, felt it against his lips. Unable to hold back, he gave her a soft kiss. When he felt her leaning into it, he pulled back slightly and pressed his advantage. "Do you want more from me, Teal?"

Her eyes widened and her hands pushed against his chest. "More what exactly, Zach? I get the feeling you're not talking about just another night of naked wrestling."

He took his hands off the crate and backed off a little. "That's because I'm not."

"You want what? A relationship?"

His raised his eyebrows. "Is that so surprising?"

"Well, yes, it is. We barely know each other."

"That's what a relationship is, getting to know each other better, in every way."

She shook her head slowly. "I don't think so, Zach. You're super sexy and I like you, but I just don't think I could ever be what you need."

It was his turn to fold his arms across his chest. That way he could be sure his pounding heart wouldn't jump straight through his ribs. This was it. He knew that if he didn't handle this right, he'd never get another shot with her. In thirty-six years he'd never wanted to have a serious, lasting relationship, but by damned if she hadn't suddenly become the most important thing to him.

"Just what is it you think I need?"

"Someone who's a lot more submissive than I'll ever be."

"You don't think you'd enjoy being submissive for me? You were willing to get on the cross last night."

She shivered and her nipples became twin points pressing against her thin blouse. It wasn't cold in there, so he knew the thought of her being on the cross was as appealing to her as it was to him.

"I've never been tied up." She shrugged. "I figured why not give it a try? But the urge has passed."

"Really?"

"Um-hmmm."

A grin tried to escape, but he held it back. He couldn't get too cocky. "You don't strike me as someone who would let fear rule her."

"What fear? Just because I enjoy my independence and don't want to call some man Master, you think I'm scared?"

"No, I think you're scared because you *do* enjoy your independence so much. Then last night, you got a taste of what it would be like to relax and let someone else be in charge once in a while, and you liked it."

"It was just good chemistry and good sex, Zach. Don't make it out to be more than it was." Her words were firm, but she knew, deep inside, that he was right. He had cooked for her, talked to her about everything and anything, and then teased and pleased her more than any man had ever before.

"You're wrong, and I can prove it to you. If you're brave enough to let me."

Damn it. He made it sound like a dare!

"How's that?" Teal leaned back against the crate and used crossing her legs as an excuse to press her thighs together. Everything inside her was heating to the melting point at the prospect of being with him again, even while her brain screamed at her that the submission thing was a slippery slope.

"Tonight, my basement, when you're done here."

He was backing away from her as he spoke, and something like panic tightened her muscles. "I've got a lot to do. I might not be done until late."

"I'll still be there." His expression got intent for a minute. "It's your choice, Teal."

Then he was gone. And Teal was alone and wound up.

13

It took just over an hour for Teal to admit to herself that Zach had been right.

The way she'd felt when just sitting in his kitchen watching him cook for her, and the way he'd teased her and made her plead for her orgasms . . . She'd loved every minute of it. She knew she wasn't, and never would be, a submissive person, but she couldn't deny she'd felt a certain intoxicating freedom with him. The thought of never experiencing it again wasn't something she wanted to contemplate.

So before she could think any more, she grabbed her purse and headed for his place. She wasn't going because he'd dared her, either.

The drive to the north side of the river went by surprisingly fast, and it was still light out when she pulled into Zach's driveway. Without slowing down, she marched up the walk and rang the bell. When the door swung open and she caught sight of him, any ability to think rationally fled.

Wearing nothing but soft leather pants, he looked deliciously decadent and completely masterful. Her breasts got heavy and her pussy throbbed while she drank in the sight of him. Light tufts of hair dusted his chest and trailed down a belly with visible ridges and valleys. Her mouth watered and she fought the urge to drop to her knees right then and there and start licking. As she looked on, the package behind the zipper swelled, and she knew he was hard everywhere.

She lifted her gaze and took in the blond hair, dark from a recent shower, which flopped over his forehead and curled around his ears, giving him the exact right amount of softness.

Oh man, I'm in trouble.

"So," she said, "show me what you're offering."

His eyebrows jumped at her abruptness, but he just smiled and opened the door wider for her. Feeling a bit like a fly about to be caught in a spider web, she stepped inside.

Without hesitating, she headed for the door to his basement and down the steps. She felt his silent presence behind her every step of the way and chastised herself. She was acting as if she was, indeed, scared, and that would not do.

Deliberately injecting into her voice a lightness she didn't feel, she spun to face him at the bottom of the steps. "Where would you like me, sir?"

His lips twitched and he stepped toward her. Before she knew what he was up to, his head dipped and he planted a fast and hard kiss on her lips, and then stepped back with a gleam in his eyes.

"That's a loaded question if I ever heard one," he chuckled. "For right now, I want you on the cross."

His wicked humor was reassuring. This wasn't going to be such a big deal, she thought as she made her way to the corner where the big cross was. It's not like he was going to pull out a paddle or cat-o'-nine-tails.

Her natural confidence surged forward again, and she strolled behind the cross. "I assume you want me naked?" Peeking at him from between the thick wooden slats, she started to peel her clothes off slowly, swaying to the Celtic music floating throughout the room.

"That does work best, but only if you're comfortable with it."

Teal's confidence surged as he stood there and watched her tease him with a little peekaboo show. His eyes fairly glowed with desire and he stood with his hands at his sides, making no effort to hide his own arousal. When she stepped out in front of the cross again, the air was thick with tension and her insides trembled with anticipation. She wanted his hands on her again so badly.

"So beautiful," he purred as he moved forward in a languid prowl. He stepped around her naked form, trailing heated fingertips up her arm, across her back, over her shoulder, and down the slope of her breast. His thumb and forefinger pinched her nipple lightly and she gasped, surprised at the intense jolt of pleasure that shot straight to her core. "It's not just the way you look that makes you beautiful. There's a fire in your eyes and an ingrained sensuality in your movements that makes me ache with desire every time I'm around you."

His words were magical, his voice almost hypnotic as his hands guided her onto the cross. The cold of the hardwood was a shock to her overheated body, but it only lasted a second, then the wood seemed to soften, as if it absorbed her heat.

She kept her eyes on him as he wrapped her wrists in wool-lined cuffs. "Too tight?" he asked, and she shook her head. He moved onto the next, and then knelt at her feet.

He cupped a large hand around the curve of her calf, and then ran his hand down to her ankle.

"Such lovely skin you have, too. So pale and soft. It was too dark for us last night. I didn't get to see your body flush all pretty and pink when your blood started to really pump. But I plan on seeing it all tonight." He looked up at her from his position between her spread thighs. Fingers walked up her leg, and her heart pounded as he got closer to her sex. "Just like I can see that you're already wet."

She'd been wet since he'd crowded her against the crate in the gallery. She closed her eyes and prayed that he wasn't planning on teasing her all night long. She wasn't sure just how long she could withstand it without caving.

She'd plead with him to fuck her, and then he'd think he could always dominate her. He'd think that he could control her.

14

Teal kept her eyes closed while she heard Zach move about. She wanted to watch what he was doing, but she knew she needed to stay inside her own head if she wanted to maintain some control.

She expected a light, teasing touch from Zach, similar to the way he'd played her body the night before. So when he stepped right up between her thighs, gripped her waist, and slanted his mouth over hers, her body reacted as if electrified. Her mouth opened for him, letting him plunder and ravage with full, intense passion as her arms flexed against the restraints in an effort to reach for him. He pressed into her, letting her feel the hardness of his erection against her sex. Her heart pounded and mewls of passion escaped at her inability to touch him.

Then he was gone.

Her eyes snapped open to see him less than a foot away from her, his lips wet, his chest rising and falling rapidly; as he watched her. "Don't close your eyes during this. I want you to see me, to never doubt that it's me who's touching you and me who's going to give you what you want. Don't shut me out by closing your eyes. Understand?"

She nodded and he leaned in and kissed her again. This time his domination was softer, but just as thorough. He tasted like mint and honey, fresh, and sweet, and potent.

"Good girl," he purred, and stepped back again. "Now, let's find out just how much you enjoy letting someone else be in charge every now and then, shall we?"

Their gazes locked, Teal saw the flare in his dark eyes when he touched her. The same flare of heat that was deep in her belly. Like they were connected.

He ran one hand up and over her rib cage, stopping just below the curve of her breast, then the other. Then his thumbs skimmed the tender skin before his hands moved up and completely covered her breasts. And he wasn't gentle.

Heat shot to her pussy as he fondled her breasts. He tweaked her nipples and she gasped. He squeezed them and she moaned. He pulled at them and she bit her lip to stay a whimper as juices flooded her core. She'd never been handled so gruffly. He was testing her, staring deep into her eyes and searching out each response to see just what effect it had on her.

He stepped back and reached for something silver and shiny from inside the armoire. A touch of unease seeped through her when he grasped one breast in his hand and slipped a rubber-tipped clamp over the nipple. Watching her eyes carefully, he released it.

Immediate pain shot through her like lightning. "No! Ouch, no!" Before the word "ouch" passed her lips he had the clamp off.

"Shhh, it's okay," he crooned. His hand covered her breast, the warmth of it soothing the nipple. "That was a little too much for you, eh?"

The twinkle in his eye made her giggle as she nodded, and the pain faded away. Still apprehensive, she watched as he adjusted the little screw on the clamp and placed it over her nipple again. Their eyes met and he released it.

Pain whipped through her again and she tensed, but it quickly eased to a dull throb. He grinned, and pleasure suffused her. He repeated the process with the other breast, this time without the too-tight first try. When both breasts were bound, he tugged lightly on the chain between them and electric heat jumped from her nipples to her clit.

"Oh!"

Zach nodded and stepped forward. He cupped a hand around her jaw and tilted her head up, giving him complete access to her throat. His lips brushed against her neck, then his tongue and his teeth. He nibbled and sucked, making shivers dance up and down her spine. Her nipples tightened, the throb in them increasing.

A warm hand slid over her belly and between her thighs and she moaned. So good, his touch was so good. He swiped a finger the length of her slit, parting her folds. The heel of his hand pressed against her aching clit and he thrust a finger inside. Then another. He rocked his hand, his fingers fucking her, his chest pressed against hers, the clamps making her extra sensitive to every brush of skin.

Her panting breath filled the room; the world fell away until there was only her, him, and their connection. He didn't need to look into her eyes anymore. Everything he did stoked the fire in her belly until her hips were pumping against his hand. She tossed her head, nudging at him, and he nipped her on the chin. Then his mouth was on hers again, and she was in heaven.

His tongue thrust into her mouth at the same time his fingers thrust deep and wiggled inside her setting off her orgasm.

Pleasure covered every one of her nerve endings and she cried out, pressing back against the cross behind her, and pulling at her restraints at the same time.

Zach pulled back slightly, and when their eyes met again, his smile was soft and . . . proud. "Beautiful."

He trailed a fingertip down her cheek to the corner of her mouth and she turned her head to kiss it. She parted her lips and sucked on it gently, heat building inside her again. She ran her tongue over it, nipped the tip with her teeth, and saw pure lust flare in his eyes.

He thrust his hips against hers. The steel ridge of his hard-on sheathed in soft leather wasn't enough. She wanted him. All of him. Now.

"Take me," she whispered.

When he pulled away she thought he was going to make her beg. But he only moved back far enough for her to see as he made quick work of his zipper. He pushed his pants low on his hips and his cock sprang free—long, thick, and red with desire.

She licked her lips as he stroked himself once, twice. The sight of him completely naked except for undone leather pants that framed his hardness as he touched himself had made her forget where she was. She reached for him, only to find she was still strapped to the cross. Before she could voice a plea or protest, he stepped forward, between her legs again.

The head of his cock nudged against her swollen folds, finding its way to her entrance; he gripped her hips before thrusting deep and true.

"Oh, yes!"

Zach rested his forehead against hers, their eyes locked, their breath mingling as he began to make love to her.

And that's what it was. She saw it and she felt it. It didn't matter that she couldn't touch him physically, that they weren't in a soft bed somewhere. What mattered was the emotion in his eyes and in her heart. For the first time ever, Teal felt a true connection with someone. A connection that was stronger than one of their bodies.

Her insides tightened, clutching at him as his pace increased and sweat dripped down his temple. The musky scent of sex filled the room, as potent and raw as the liquid sounds of flesh slapping against flesh.

Zach reached up and tugged sharply at the chain between her breasts, pulling the clips from both nipples. Pain and pleasure flashed straight to her core and she came. Her cunt tightened around him and her body shuddered as the world tilted and went out of focus.

When she came back to reality, Zach remained inside her, frozen in position. She smiled, a languid heat making her mellow. "Thank you," she said.

"My pleasure," he replied.

He reached down, and with a flick of his wrist, one leg was free, then the other. Without another word he started moving again. Both his hands slipped behind her, under her ass, tilting her hips forward for deeper penetration. She curled her back, wrapped her legs around his waist, and held on for the ride.

Teal didn't think she could come again. She didn't need to. She just wanted to make it good for him, to enjoy the feel of Zack's cock stroking in and out of her, the connection they'd built.

She tightened her inner muscles and he groaned, his expression one of pure glory. "So good," he panted. "You feel so good. So right."

He pumped his hips and sweat trickled down his temple as he met her gaze. There was pleasure, pride, and a touch of awe there.

Her chest tightened and her heart pounded. Her throat closed up and she had to bite her tongue. She was in love with him. How the hell it had happened so quickly she had no idea, but in that moment, the connection was so strong and so clear, she knew it was love.

As if he could read her thoughts, his eyes widened and his grip on her tightened. He gasped, his body arching as he thrust deep and held her tight. He threw back his head and groaned as his cock swelled and pulsed, emptying everything he had into her.

The liquid heat spread from him to her, and to her surprise, her inner sex clenched and ripples of pleasure radiated through her in a third orgasm. She tightened her legs around his waist, and he pressed his full body against her, burying his face in her neck as they both fought to catch their breath and come down to earth.

Zach held her to him with one hand and stretched up to release her wrists. When she was free, she let her legs fall and he lowered her back to the ground, slipping from her body.

"Teal?" he questioned as he straightened up.

"Shhh"—she pressed a finger against his lips—"Let's go to bed now."

15

The sharp shriek of the phone jarred Zach from a deep sleep. Trying not to wake Teal, he stretched out an arm and snagged the phone before it could call out again.

"Zach? I'm sorry to wake you, but is Teal there? She's not answering her home phone or her cell." Brina Jo's voice was slightly panicked.

"Yeah, she's sleeping. Is everything okay?"

Her sigh came through the phone lines loud and clear. "Well, I'm glad to see you two are working things out . . . You are, right? This is the start of something, and not just a two-night stand or something, right?"

"Brina Jo? Is this why you called?"

Teal lifted her head and looked around. "Brina Jo?"

He rubbed her back with one hand. "She's on the phone, sweetheart." The endearment slipped out naturally as he pressed the unit to her ear.

"What? Brina? What's wrong?" Her voice was groggy and the frown heavy on her forehead when she sat up and took hold of the phone. His woman was clearly not a morning person.

Okay, maybe five-thirty was a little early for a lot of people, but still, she looked real cranky. Good to know for the future.

"What?" Her body tensed as she snapped the word out, dragging his attention from her naked breasts. "Nooooo. They caught him? Okay. Yes, I'll be right there."

She jumped from the bed and threw the phone into his lap. "I've gotta go."

He put the phone back in its cradle and threw the sheets back. "What happened?"

"Someone broke into the gallery and trashed it. Well, Brina Jo said their plan was to trash it, but the cops got there before too much damage was done. I have to go. Where are my clothes?" She threw her hands up. "Fuck!"

She dashed from the room and her footsteps thumped down the stairs to the basement.

A white-hot flash of anger went through Zach at the thought of someone deliberately doing damage to all that Teal had worked for. Closing his eyes, he took a deep breath, then another. Now was not the time to be angry, now was the time to be there for her . . . for the woman he was in love with.

He tugged on a pair of jeans, and T-shirt in hand, he met Teal in the living room.

"What more can fucking happen? Why me? Why now? This gallery is a *good* idea, damn it, and I can't even get it opened!" She was cursing fiercely while she fought with a shoe and he couldn't handle it anymore.

"Hey, hey, hey." He reached out and pulled her against his chest. Stroking his fingers through her hair, he tried to soothe her. "It's okay. They caught whoever it was, and Brina said there wasn't much damage, right? We can fix whatever it is in time for the opening."

She pushed back from him. "What do you mean *we* can fix the damage?"

His chest tightened at the anger in her eyes, and he had to remind himself that it wasn't him she was angry with. "Just what I said. I'll come with you, help you get things cleaned up."

She shook her head and avoided his eyes, putting her shoes on. "That's not necessary. It's my place, not yours, and I'll deal with it."

"I know it's not necessary, but I'd like to do it."

She straightened up and started for the door. "Just because I let you be in charge when we get naked doesn't mean you are in charge of everything I do. This is my place, and I said I'd handle it."

"I know it's your place, and I'm not trying to control you. I just want to help you." Impatience and hurt crept into his voice and she snapped at him.

"Really? You want to help me? Then get out of my way so I can leave."

Pain knifed through his chest. This was why she was trouble. This was why he'd known he shouldn't get involved with her. He thought he was standing beside her, and she thought he was standing in front of her, blocking her way.

He took two steps and opened the front door for her. Trying one last time as she walked past him and out the door, he said. "You don't have to deal with this alone, Teal."

But she just kept walking, without saying a word.

16

Teal was just starting to think she'd overreacted. That she'd taken her anger at the vandals out on Zach because he was closest, when she walked in the gallery and saw Dominick talking to a police officer at the reception desk.

"Teal!" Brina Jo called out from the middle of the gallery. She left her husband, who she'd been hugging, and came rushing over. "I know it looks bad, but I've looked around, and it looks lots worse than it is."

She stood still while Brina Jo gave her a hard and fast hug.

The beautiful cream walls were decorated with the words "sinners," "slut," "whore," all in neon green and yellow. The corner section where she'd placed the glass dildo, along with some stained glass frames of couples in the throes of passion, was smashed apart. There was toilet paper strewn from one end of the room to the other. She saw a hole in the north wall where someone had thrown the heavy brass-plated sculpture that now lay on the floor.

"Not that bad, huh?"

Small but firm fingers gripped her chin and forced her to look into Brina's face. "It really isn't. Nothing a little paint and elbow grease won't fix."

Afraid that if she let herself feel relief, she'd burst into tears, Teal gave Brina Jo a sharp nod and a small smile. Then she turned to face her brother. With every step she took toward the reception desk, she became more aware of her rapidly over-loading emotions.

"What are you doing here, Dominick?"

"Lacey called me when they caught the kids in here and they couldn't get hold of you." His amber eyes flashed, but his lips curved up in a smile for the female in uniform leaning against the desk. "I called Brina Jo and came down to check on things."

It was a reasonable explanation. She hadn't been at home, and her cell phone had been with her clothes in Zach's base-ment. Except, it was Brina Jo's name listed on everything as her assistant for the gallery.

Teal glanced at the pretty young police officer who only had eyes for Dom. She crossed her arms, trying to hold her temper in. "So she's your friend who told you about the graffiti, huh?"

The cop's posture straightened and the happy light in her eyes dimmed. She held out her hand for Teal and spoke up for herself. "I'm Officer Young, Ms. Jamison. I just want to let you know that the two guys responsible for this are in custody and that, judging by the tags on the walls, it's the same ones who were decorating the outside of your building lately. You shouldn't have any more trouble, because they won't be back."

"Thank you. Although I'd appreciate it if, in the future, there is ever a need to contact me about my business, you do it your-self, or through my assistant. Not my brother."

"Yes, ma'am."

"Did you need anything else here?" Teal asked.

"No, ma'am. Your assistant has a copy of the police report,

and she assured us she'd get a list of the damages in the next day or two."

"Thank you, then." Teal spoke briskly and the girl got the hint.

With a smile and a wave at Dominick, she said good-bye. "I hope your day gets better, ma'am."

"You were a little hard on her, don't you think?" Dom walked around the desk to stand in front of Teal. "After all, it's not her fault she couldn't get a hold of you right away."

"No, it's not," Teal snapped. "But it is her fault that she called you instead of doing what she should've done, what a professional would've done, and called the name on the business contact sheets."

"She was doing me a favor, Teal. I asked her to keep an eye on the place, to see if you were right and it was just punk kids, or if there was someone more sinister harassing my little sister."

"And I was right, wasn't I? It was just punks getting a cheap thrill." She threw her hands up in the air, wanting to smack him. "I can look after myself, Dominick. I don't need you babying me all the time!"

"I wasn't babying you, damn it! I was just concerned!"

"Well, I don't need your concern either."

His brows drew down in a fierce frown and he glared at her. "That's right, you don't need anyone or anything, do you, Teal? How the hell did you get to be such a selfish control freak? Mom and Dad raised us to be a family, to care about one another. And that means being there when someone is hurt."

"It's not selfish to want to run my own life my own way! Or my business, for that matter!"

"Have I tried to tell you how to run your life or your business? No! I just wanted to make sure you were safe. Jesus, Teal, relax, would you?"

Teal stood there, hands clenched in fists as she faced off with her brother. They both had tempers, and fighting was nothing new to them. But this time it seemed she was the only one fighting.

"I'm sorry, Dom." She took a deep breath, shook out her hands, and tried to smile at him. "You know I love you, you're my family. I've just been a bit tense lately. I've built a lot of businesses from the ground up, but this is the first one that's *mine*. It's really important to me."

"I know it is." He grinned, then pulled her against his chest in a hard hug and kissed her forehead. "God bless the poor sap who falls in love with you, because he's going to need the patience of a saint."

17

It took less than an hour for Teal to realize that she just might be able to get everything cleaned up and ready for the gallery's opening on Friday. It would be a lot of work, but mostly it was grunt work that anyone could do.

Two of the display shelves Zach had put in had been ripped out of the walls, but the wood was undamaged, and after the walls were patched and repainted they could be reinstalled.

She just needed to call Zach and ask him if he'd do it.

"Have a nice day."

Teal gave her head a shake and pasted a smile on her face. With a polite thank you, she picked up the party box full of donuts and muffins and the tray of gourmet coffees and headed out the door. Five minutes later, she pulled up in front of the gallery and tried to calm her heartbeat as she stared at Zach's truck, already parked in the lot.

Throwing back her shoulders, she strode into the place like she didn't want to run straight to him and apologize for her outburst that morning. She saw him immediately, standing in the south corner of the room with a full bag of trash between him and her brother.

They both looked her way when she arrived, but neither waved or said anything. Teal's gaze slid away from Zach's unreadable one to see a shit-eating grin on her brother's face. The sinking sensation in the pit of her stomach made her want to run and hide.

"How long have they been like that?" Teal asked Brina Jo, who'd joined her and was already munching on a Boston cream.

Brina eyed her and swallowed before answering. "Since Zach got here."

"And that was how long ago?"

"About five minutes after you walked out the door." There was a beat of silence as the women stared at each other. "I'm a bit surprised he didn't show up with you earlier, actually."

Heat crept up Teal's neck. "He wanted to, but I, um . . . told him to back off."

Her friend frowned and picked up two of the coffees. "I can't say I'm surprised. Disappointed, but not surprised."

Teal stood there, her heart pounding and her throat tightening as Brina carried the coffees over to her husband.

Doug had canceled his own workday to help out. Dom, like Doug, had gone home and showered before giving up his appointments to stick around and do cleanup.

They all knew Lush was her baby, and they all cared about her enough to help her get it back in shape. She hadn't even had to ask.

Finally, Teal let her gaze rest on Zach.

He looked good. Calm, cool, and collected as he talked to Dom. His hair was in its natural, slightly mussed state, and he was dressed to work. As if nothing had happened.

Something grabbed hold of Teal's heart and started to squeeze.

He had let her walk out that morning. He'd let her deal with the immediate crisis without trying to take over. She knew now that he'd only wanted to be there for her, the same way her brother was. The same way her friends were.

Despite Zach's admitted fondness for sexual domination, he'd never once tried to force her into anything, or take any type of choice away from her. She glanced back at the photo behind her. It was miraculously untouched, and she was thankful, because now she could see something she'd missed before.

That photo matched what Zach had said to her in the basement. The submissive one was the one ultimately in control. The man wasn't dominating her so much as she was gifting him with her submission.

Zach didn't dominate her, or try to control her. He just accepted what trust she gave. And he would never take something she wasn't willing to give.

Zach tried not to stare when Teal strode into the gallery. She looked amazing. But something was missing. The magic that was her, the attitude that had both caught his attention and warned him away, was gone. Heaviness settled in the pit of his gut when their gazes met and hers skittered away quickly.

Was she pissed off to see him there?

"You have got your hands full, don't you?" Dom laughed at him in a way that only a man who's never been in love could.

Zach met Teal's brother's gaze. It hadn't taken five seconds for Dominick to put two and two together when he'd walked in the gallery only to find Teal had left to shower.

"So you're the reason no one could get hold of my sister this morning, eh?" had been the way Dominick had greeted him.

He'd looked Dom straight in the eyes and said, "Yes. Do you have a problem with your sister having a private life?"

At first Zach thought the guy was going to swing at him, but he was pleasantly surprised when, instead, Dom had grinned and clapped him on the shoulder.

They'd gotten started cleaning up, working side by side, with Dom grilling him not so subtly about himself and his relationship with Teal. Zach had answered the questions about himself, but stonewalled him when it came to Teal and their relationship.

But this time he just answered with the simple truth, "I'm in love with her."

He saw Dom's eyes flick over his shoulder and he knew Teal was standing behind him. Before he could turn to her, she was at his side.

"Take this and get lost," she said, holding out a steaming paper cup to her brother.

Dominick took the cup and walked away without a word. Zach turned to Teal, bracing himself for her anger. She could yell at him all she wanted for being there, but he wasn't leaving.

Teal shoved her hands in the back pockets of her jeans to keep from grabbing Zach and kissing him. Sure, he'd shown up, but it might just be because he still had one podium to finish for her. The closed look on his face was one she'd never seen before and she didn't like it.

Unsure of exactly what to say, she started at the top. "Thank you."

His eyes widened and his mouth opened to speak, but she put a hand out to stop him. "Please, let me say what I need to say before I lose my nerve."

His jaw snapped shut and he nodded, a small light flickering in the depths of his eyes.

"Thank you for letting me go this morning, for letting me come here alone, *and* for showing up now. It means a lot to see you here." She took a deep breath, shaking her head at him when he opened his mouth again. "Also, I want to say I'm sorry. I was a bit of a bitch this morning, when all you were trying to do was help."

When she didn't continue, he raised his eyebrows and she nodded.

"A bit of a bitch?" His eyes sparkled and lips twitched.

"Yeah, well, I'm not much of a morning person."

He chuckled and pulled her to him in a hug. "I gathered that."

Teal relaxed into him. She couldn't believe it had been that easy. That Zach wasn't going to make her beg for his forgiveness. He felt so good, so solid and comforting. His cotton T-shirt was soft beneath her cheek. His clean, crisp scent filled her lungs, and his heartbeat thumped steadily against her ear.

Being in his arms felt so right, and she finally accepted that, yes, being together could be that easy. That was the whole thing. Zach truly wanted only what she was willing to give.

She leaned back and looked up at him, stilling his arms. "I have more to say."

His arms tightened around her, but he nodded. "Okay, go ahead."

"I was scared."

Her insides trembled and she locked her knees, hoping she wouldn't collapse if he pulled away. He didn't pull away. In fact, he pulled her closer, so their bodies pressed together from knees to chest. "I know," he said softly. "But I don't want you to ever be scared of me. In any way."

"Enough already, you two. Get to work, would you?" Dom's voice echoed through the gallery, followed by Brina Jo's and Doug's laughter.

Before Teal could step back, Zach sank his fingers into her

hair and pulled her head back. His eyes shining with emotion, he brought his mouth down on hers and kissed her thoroughly for all to see. When he lifted his head again her knees were weak, and the look in his eyes made her heart expand with emotion.

She'd finally found her niche.

"Everything looks perfect."

A shiver danced down Teal's spine at the husky words spoken into her ear. Zach spread his hand across her belly and pulled her back against him. She could feel his hard-on against her butt and wiggled against it as she stared out at the people milling about Lush.

He was right. The opening was a success.

Her parents had flown in from Victoria the day before to help get everything ready. And they'd brought some impressive erotic paintings to be displayed. They wouldn't tell her who the artist was, but she had a sneaking suspicion it was her mother.

"It does look good, doesn't it?" She leaned back into Zach's arms. "We did it."

"You did it." He kissed her neck.

"With help from my friends." She grinned.

Dominick was standing about ten feet away from them with Wanda Brooks, the blond columnist from his paper. She'd been super nice to Teal, but she was tearing a strip off of Dom about something and Teal knew she owed him.

Brina and Doug were standing by the temporary bar chatting with Doug's cousin, the last-minute caterer. Several artists had made it a point to be there for the opening, and they were mingling with clients. Sales for the day already totaled the first three months of operating expenses, and Teal knew it was just the beginning.

She laced her fingers through Zach's hand and led him to the back room. She walked down the short aisle and pulled him behind a large stack of wooden packing crates. Without a word, she pinned him to the wall and kissed him.

She put her whole heart into the kiss. Zach's hands cupped her ass and he pulled her tight to him. He spun around quickly and pinned her to the wall. Pulling his mouth from hers, he kissed his way along her jaw and nipped at her earlobe with his teeth.

"You are so naughty," he purred.

"And you love that I'm so lusty." She slid her hand between their bodies and stroked him through his pants.

"No," he said, pulling back slightly. He gazed into her eyes, completely serious. "I love you. Period."

Teal's heart kicked in her chest and a minute trembling started within her. "It's only been a week, Zach."

"I know. But I knew from the moment I met you that you were special. You challenge me, you inspire me, and you let me tie you up." He grinned at her and she knew his words were true. "I love your independence, I love your brain and your body. . . . I love *you*, Teal."

"So you're telling me it's more than lust, huh?" She whispered.

"So much more."

"Good." She met his gaze and let him see what was in her heart. "Because I don't ever plan on letting you go, even if I have to tie *you* up."

Passion Play

1

Mia

I was in hell.

Okay, it wasn't literally hell, it was a coffee shop. But it felt like hell. And the icy blonde across from me was the devil.

"What do you mean you're done?" I rubbed the silver snake ring on my middle left finger with my thumb. The smooth cool metal was solid and comforting.

"Your stuff isn't moving, Mia, and as much as I like you, this is my business. I have to make smart decisions."

"You like me? Sharon, you're my cousin! You came to *me* with the idea of marketing and selling my jewelry. I quit my job to build an inventory because you told me we could do this. You told me you could sell ice to an Eskimo. That's what you said. Ice to an Eskimo."

"I'm sorry, Mia. I've tried, but no one is interested in your stuff. It's just too . . . unusual."

I folded my arms across my chest to stop from grabbing the bitch and shaking her. "You said that's why it would sell. Because it's unique!"

The ice queen raised a slim penciled-in eyebrow and shrugged delicately. "I'm sorry, but I've tapped all my sources, and no one is interested."

"So you were wrong." Pressure built inside my head. I wasn't pissed so much about her not being able to sell my stuff as much as the way she acted. Like none of it was her idea, her fault. Nothing was ever her fault.

Her thin lips pursed tight. "The timing is wrong."

I stared at her and counted to ten in my head, breathing long, deep breaths. It didn't help.

Leaning forward, I spoke softly, my words all the more forceful in their quietness. "You selfish little bitch. You can't even admit you were wrong. It's pathetic."

I clenched my jaw, holding the rest back. Sharon wasn't worth it. She was just a brittle bottle blonde who didn't care about anyone but herself. I should really feel sorry for her. With a shake of my head I turned and stalked out of the shop.

So much for family.

Not that I'd ever truly felt a part of the Jones clan.

The Jones family. Can you get any duller than that? Sadly, my extended family lived up to the name, or should I say down to it?

Either way, they were boring.

I was used to being the black sheep with them. Even before I got my first piercing, my aunt and uncle didn't have a clue how to handle me. My parents had always encouraged me to be my own person. They'd encouraged me to never let other people's misconceptions keep me from doing anything. So, when I was four and had wanted to shave my hair off to look like Dad, they took me to the barbershop and had it done.

At seven years old, I'd wanted to play baseball in a town where there was no girls team and Mom and Dad had fought the town council to let me play on the boys team.

Two years later, they died in a car accident and I went to live with my aunt and uncle, my mom's sister and her husband. They were blood, but they never really accepted me as family. I was alone.

None of them had ever been risk-takers; none of them had ever really understood me. According to them, I was too much of a smart-mouth with an attitude. They'd never even tried to see below the surface.

That, of course, had made me want to make the surface just a bit more outrageous. I admit it. But what started out as rebellion helped me find my way to what I loved best: silver crafting unique and edgy jewelry. I'd been content to work as a receptionist at a construction company until Sharon had come up with the brilliant plan of making my hobby into a business.

I should've known better than to trust her, cousin or not.

2

Dominick

I glared at the pages in my hand so hard they started to blur into a sea of red. I wished for laser eyesight so they'd burn up from the heat. Hell, if I had laser eyesight, it wouldn't be the pages I'd be using it on, but the individual who'd decided to mess with them.

"What's wrong, Nick? You forget how to spell misogynistic? Oh, wait! That's one word you'll *never* forget, right?"

I ignored the bitter blonde and she walked away in a huff. Wanda Brooks would never forgive me for not wanting to go past date one with her, let alone being a vocal supporter of the right to stay single.

Not that it really mattered to me, the Society/Arts columnist was good-looking, even charming when she wanted to be, but she'd been interested in Nick, the quasi-celebrity, not Dominick, the person. And I was past the point of just wanting to get laid so I had notches on my belt.

"Nick at Night" is my weekly column in the paper. A column that talks to men about what's happening in the city, where's a good place to take a date, and often, what warning signs to watch for in a female determined to get to the altar. Full of sports analogies that are easy to understand, it's a "man about town" sort of thing.

It had made me popular with men, not always so popular with women.

Judging by all the red the new editor had inserted into my latest offering, Wanda wasn't the only one trying to change things. Slapping the pages against my thigh as I walked, I headed for the editor's office. I tried to calm the anger simmering in my gut.

I didn't bother knocking when I reached the door marked EDITOR IN CHIEF. I just walked in and closed the door behind me with deliberate gentleness.

"Since when do you tell me what to put in my column?"

"Nick, come in, sit down. What's on your mind?"

I stared at the guy behind the shiny new glass and chrome desk and felt a throbbing behind my eyes. As of three months ago, Terrance Jacobs was *The City*'s new editor in chief, and a brainless asshole.

"What's on my mind?" I fought to keep my voice calm. "Since when does anyone rewrite my column?"

"Rewrite your column? No one's done that."

Terrance leaned back in his chair with a suitably perplexed look. A complete fake one.

I held up the sheets with the new paragraphs added in red pencil and waved it around. "No? This isn't the column I wrote. This is a sales ad for that new restaurant downtown."

"It's hardly an ad, Nick. I just added a mention for the place. After all, you did eat there the other night, didn't you?"

"Yes, I did. And it sucked," I said bluntly. "Which is why I didn't mention it myself. My readers trust what I say, and I want to keep it that way."

"Well, I ate there yesterday and it was superb. They also bought six months' worth of ad space from us, so I think an extra mention here and there is good business."

"Nick at Night" is good business, and it's that way because I don't advertise just any place that pays out or gives perks. I've earned a reputation as an honest guy. When I recommend a place, it's good. You're not going to fuck that up." Didn't the guy get it?

The City had started out as a weekly eclectic underground newspaper full of information about life in Edmonton. It contained everything from entertainment to opinionated columns about local politics. It had built up and developed a devoted following due to the fact that it told things as it was. Entertainment, food reviews, political debates, and human-interest stories—all the things that the bigger papers didn't cover, or were scared to be openly honest and opinionated about.

Things had been great; most of the staff respected each other and their areas of expertise, even if they didn't always get along. Then the owner decided to try and go more mainstream, and he'd hired Terrance, who liked to pretend he was a "person for the people," when really he was a snake oil salesman.

"I'm the editor. What I say goes in the paper, goes in the paper." His phony smile was just a bit too cocky for me. My temper hit its boiling point and I gritted my teeth. I did not want this asshole knowing he got to me.

I swallowed my retort and glared at him.

Then a strange calm settled in the pit of my stomach and I gave Terrance a tight smile. It was that time. "Fine."

I left the office and went straight to my computer. This wasn't the time to second-guess myself. It took about ten minutes to whip out a new column and print it. Clean papers in hand, I dashed down to the production department.

"Tom, I have a last-minute change for my column. Can you put this one in tomorrow's issue instead of the scheduled one?"

The old man who had been the paper's printer at the beginning, and who still did layouts the old way while his assistants did the same work digitally, wiped his ink-stained hands and reached for the sheet. He scanned it, then looked up at me with raised eyebrows. "I can't say I didn't see this coming. Has Jacobs seen it?"

The production manager was a shrewd man. I shook my head. Would Tom print the public resignation, or would he refuse without the boss's permission?

"Okay, Dom. It'll be in tomorrow's slot . . . if you're sure?"

Relief made my muscles slack. "I'm sure. Thanks, buddy."

The early evening sun felt great beating down on my shoulders as I strolled through the small park area that separated the new offices from where I'd had to park. Parking along Whyte Avenue wasn't easy to find, especially with all the shops and businesses on the street. But at least the warm September made it an easy walk to the lot.

My mind was quiet as I walked . . . peaceful. There was no regret for what I'd just done. It felt pretty damn good, actually. Better than I'd ever thought possible. Writing was my addiction, but Tom was right; it had been a long time coming. For the first time in the three months since Terrance had taken over the paper, I felt human again. Like I could finally move forward.

The question was, forward to where? I'd never been unemployed before.

Forget it. I refused to think about that right now. Tonight, I'd celebrate.

Only my brain wouldn't cooperate. Options and ideas flowed steadily. There were plenty of things I could do. Tons of local papers and magazines I could write for, or maybe even write that novel I'd always wanted to write.

My gut clenched at that thought. Nah, I wasn't ready to tackle that yet. I'd start looking into other periodicals tomorrow. Maybe even try some freelance work for some men's magazines. The work is always out there.

If worst came to worst, there was always Teal's gallery. I could sell erotic art. Hell, I could sell anything if I had to.

Suddenly, a bundle of curves hit me head-on, the world tilted, and I was flat on my back before I could blink. The air jumped from my lungs in a swift rush, and something hard smacked into my mouth.

"Ouch!"

I squinted at the female cry of pain and tried to catch my breath. The soft bundle of warm, wiggling curves on top of me wasn't helping matters any. A soft moan made my dick twitch and I sucked on my bruised bottom lip.

When I could breathe again, I shifted so that the sun was blocked by the armload of sweet-smelling woman and focused on her face.

Smooth, fair skin, plump red, cock-sucking lips, diamond stud in her left nostril, and eyes that were so dark they looked black. Eyes that held the same shock I felt.

"Ouch. My head and your chin are not a good match." She chuckled.

Her breath was a sweet breeze across my lips, and I was suddenly acutely aware of the way she straddled my hips.

"Hel-lo," I said softly.

She stilled. Our eyes locked and I saw awareness dawn in hers. Then they started to sparkle. *Damn, she's hot!*

She put a finger to my lip. "Are you okay?"

"Nothing a kiss wouldn't fix."

A delicate eyebrow arched and I waited for her to smack me one. Instead, her lips tilted up at one corner and she lowered her head slowly.

Oh, yeah. I lifted up to meet her, my mouth inexorably drawn to hers.

Soft, plump lips pressed against mine; my blood heated and my body tightened as our tongues tangled. Hot and wet, she tasted of caramel and whipped cream. She pressed her hips against me and my cock throbbed, eager to get in on the action. I ran one hand up the curve of her spine and the other down to cup a firm ass.

She tore her mouth away to nuzzle against my neck and a shiver ripped down my spine. Her head tilted to get better access and the sun blinded me . . . along with the knowledge of where we were.

I groaned. Shit, we were in the middle of the park.

"Uhmm." I tried to speak, but her tongue in my ear made it difficult to think, let alone talk. I slid my hand to the back of her head, tangled my fingers in her silky hair, and tugged.

"Ooh!" she cooed as she came away, the sound making me wish we didn't have to stop.

Our eyes met and the heat there made my fist clench with the urge to pull her hair again. To flip her over and tangle my hands in her hair, spread her thighs, and plunge home.

A rowdy cry of "Get a room, would ya?" made her sit up and flip off the passerby. A chuckle built inside me at her actions and I shifted, unable to not press up against her warmth. A woman after my own heart.

"I think I'm in love," I said.

She looked down at me, planted her hands on my chest, and pushed to her feet.

She laughed, shaking her head in a way that made her red hair dance like flames in the sunlight. "That's really too bad, because I don't do love."

3

Mia

With a slight pang of regret, I waved to the hot guy I'd fallen into and walked away.

"Wait! Where are you going?" he called out.

I didn't bother looking back.

I'd been good and pissed off before the kid on the skateboard almost knocked me on my ass, but that sizzling kiss had righted the world again. Sharon might've been the one to push me into focusing on my silver crafting, but I wasn't a quitter.

The seed had been planted, and the idea cemented in my brain. No guts, no glory; no risk, no reward. It was time to go after what I wanted, and I wanted to be a jewelry designer. I wanted to see my stuff on display and hear my name spoken in reverence.

Okay, so maybe reverence was pushing it a bit, but why dream if you're not going to dream big?

And really, what's the point in chasing small dreams?

Footsteps sounded behind me a split second before a large hand clasped my arm and sent a ripple of electricity through my body.

"Hey, don't run away," said the hot guy I'd just climbed off of.

"I'm not running away, I'm leaving. There's a difference." I tried not to notice the appreciation in his eyes as they ran over me. They were such a light brown they were almost amber. Molten amber. I also tried not to notice the way his dark hair was slightly unruly, as if my fingers had just run through it.

Uh-oh. Stop drooling.

I did a mental head shake and refocused. Dreams. Chasing dreams. Jewelry design. No time for men or relationships right now, no matter how hot and sexy the guy.

"You were moving pretty fast, looked like running away to me." He shrugged, momentarily distracting me from my dream-chasing with his broad shoulders. "It's not nice to jump on a guy and then run away, you know?"

He was certainly tall, dark, and handsome, though. The body that had been between my thighs only seconds ago was one made of lean muscle that would look real good naked and covering my own. The way he'd tugged on my hair and cradled my body had made arousal snake through me at lightning speed. His body had responded to our contact, too; the press of his arousal had made my sex throb, hungry for attention.

His words sunk in, and exasperated with myself, I spoke a bit sharply. "I didn't *jump* on you. I fell when some punk going too fast on a skateboard knocked me off balance."

"Uh-huh. And you kissed me because it was the polite thing to do, right?"

His grin was charming and my pulse kicked up a notch. Whether it was because of temper or attraction, I wasn't a hundred percent sure. "I kissed you because you *asked* me to!"

"Oh, I like that," he stepped closer, invading my personal space just enough that his faintly spicy scent tickled my nose. "Does that mean you'll do everything I ask you to do?"

Oh, I liked this guy—playful, sexy, and a little devilish. Attraction won the battle, hands down. Except . . . I still needed to focus.

Bad boys would always be around to play with, but I had only a limited amount of savings left, so that meant a limited amount of time to chase the dream. And chasing dreams was too demanding to let myself get distracted by some hottie for more than a few minutes.

I looked at him from under my lashes and slowly licked my lips. When I spoke, my voice was husky with promise. "In your dreams, lover boy."

Feeling better than I had in a long, long time, I spun on my heel and strode away. And I wasn't disappointed when he didn't follow this time. Honest.

4

Mia

"Wow! You don't usually have such a glow-on after you visit your family. What's up?"

I planted my butt on the stool at the pristine juice bar next to my best friend and gave her a wicked smile. "I just told Sharon off, and then jumped on a hot guy in the park."

Caitlyn stopped trimming the tray of lemongrass in front of her and snapped to attention, her white blonde mop of curls bouncing about her face. She clapped her hands together and grinned broadly. "You told her off? Really? No wonder your aura's so bright!"

Funny how she'd glommed on to the tell-my-cousin-off thing but didn't blink at my jumping a hot guy in the park. Sometimes I wondered if Caitlyn Ellis knew me too well.

Hell, who was I kidding? I loved that someone knew me so well. Having Caitlyn as my friend and confidante was the only thing that kept me sane at times. Especially since most people thought Caitlyn herself was a little wacky.

That's what I loved about her. It's what had drawn us together when we were in school. We'd both been teen misfits in an upper middle class Catholic school. Me with my blue spiked hair and piercings before they were popular, and Caitlyn with her aura reading and openly cosmic belief system.

I didn't doubt that Caitlyn saw auras and felt people's energy. She was supersensitive to a person's pain, mental or physical, and she always tried to help them. And she'd helped me learn to deal with my adoptive family over and over again.

In return, I gave her open acceptance and love . . . and anything else I could. I loved my spirit sister. She was my true family.

"Tell me all about it. Leave no details out." Cait's blue eyes sparkled with wicked glee.

"You done for the day?" I glanced around the empty reception area.

Caitlyn was a massage therapist and the holistic clinic she worked that also hosted a psychic and an acupuncturist. When you walk in, instead of a reception desk, there was a juice bar.

"Last client is just getting cleaned up; as soon as he's gone, I'm clear for the night."

"Can I have one of those mocha smoothies while we wait?" I pasted my best "good girl" expression on my face.

Technically, there wasn't supposed to be any caffeine on the premises, but Caitlyn kept a hidden stash.

She was a believer in energy, vibes, and auras and such, but she was also a big believer in caffeine. She jumped off her stool and walked around the counter to make the smoothie. She pulled a plastic container from under the counter and quirked an eyebrow at me. "Details?"

I told her about Sharon and how the conversation with her had gone. And about how the punk had just about run me over in the park.

"So you didn't jump the guy, someone pushed you into him?" She placed a paper cup in front of me with a straw.

Just then a tall, blond, Greek god look-alike came from the back room and waved good-bye to Caitlyn. My jaw dropped and saliva pooled in my mouth. "You just gave *him* a massage?"

Cait smirked. "Ben is a regular of mine. Once a week like clockwork."

"And you've never told me about him. Why?"

"What's to tell, Mia? I don't date clients, you know that." She waved her hand in the air. "Now, tell me about the hot guy in the park."

"I could date your clients, though, right?" I gave my head a shake and focused on Caitlyn's words. "Him? Well, yeah, he was very hot. He had these gorgeous eyes. Brown, but so light that they looked like a topaz, or amber. Yeah, definitely amber."

"He's the one for you, Mia. I just know it."

"Nah." I shrugged and took a long suck on the straw. "He was just a guy."

"But the way you met, the universe was at work, giving you something to balance out what Sharon had just taken away from you by throwing you into his arms."

The tiny hairs on the back of my neck stood on end and goose bumps rose on my arms. I hated it when that happened! Sometimes Caitlyn was down right eerie.

"Stop it right there," I said. "The universe didn't throw me into his arms, I fell."

"No such thing as a coincidence," she sing-songed.

I needed to get her off the man track. If I didn't, she might actually get me to admit that I'd been mentally kicking my own ass for walking away from the hot guy. Then she'd never let me live it down.

"Besides, Sharon didn't take anything away from me. I decided I don't need her to sell my stuff. Who better to sell my jewelry than people who love it? People who believe in me. People like me . . . and you."

She reached for my hand, her big blue eyes full of concern. "Sweetie, I'd love to sell your stuff for you, but I have no contacts in retail stores, and you know sales just is not my thing."

"I know. I don't have the retail contacts either, which is why I decided to do this another way. Sharon said the stores weren't interested because my stuff was too 'different' and too 'edgy,' so I think I need to think differently." I set my empty cup on the counter and gave her a big smile. "I want you to sell some here."

At first Caitlyn's face was blank. Then her eyes lit up and she ran around the counter.

"Mia! You're brilliant! It's perfect!" She pulled me off the stool and into a hug. "Vesna's been looking for a way to bring in more people. Adding your jewelry up here would be great. I can even offer piercing services if she wants!"

Relief flowed over me, then excitement ripped through my bones. "Really? You think it's a good idea? That she'll go for it?" Vesna was the owner of the clinic. Without her say so, it would never happen.

Caitlyn grinned, reached behind the counter for her purse, and said, "I do. I think she'll love it. Let's go celebrate!"

5

Dominick

It took only one look.

My gut clenched and my blood heated in instant recognition. The way she moved, the way the flashing lights made her hair look like it was alive with fire. It was definitely her, the woman who had run over me only hours earlier and then walked away.

The woman whose kiss I could not get off of my mind.

Propping my elbow on the bar, I ignored the obvious interest from the blond cutie five feet away and watched my mystery woman dance. She was sleek and sensual, every movement striking a sexual cord deep within me. Her small breasts jiggled, her hips circled, and her skirt rose up on strong, muscular thighs with each gyration. But it was her face that captured me the most.

Her eyes closed, she danced in her own world with the music. She lifted the hair off the back of her neck, then let it fall, one hand stretching up while the other trailed over the gleaming skin of her neck and collarbone. I watched her suck a full bottom lip between little white teeth and swivel her hips again.

She looked like she was fucking someone. Like it was someone else's hands running over her body, putting that expression of pure pleasure on her face.

Blood flowed south and my cock swelled and pressed against my zipper. She needed a dance partner; no woman like that should be alone.

I reached back and set down my barely touched beer before pushing off from the bar, only to see another guy move in on her.

Fuck!

The newcomer was just a kid, barely twenty-one. Something ugly settled in my gut. I'd gotten a pretty good look at her up close and she had to be closer to thirty. It couldn't be her date, but she hadn't pulled away from the kid, and the way they moved together to the music said she wasn't running from him.

"Hey, Jimmy," I called the bartender over. "You know her?"

Jimmy looked in the direction I was watching and grinned knowingly. "Who, Mia? Yeah, I know her."

I gave him a look. "Well?"

"What do you want to know?"

"Everything you know. What's her story?"

"Not much, man. Mia's an open book, but those pages are blank."

No way. "You mean she's a bimbo?"

"No!" Jimmy shook his head and waved off the other bartender. "I mean she's open, friendly, and just a bit wild on the outside. But she keeps the rest hidden. She'll show you anything and do almost anything on a dare, but she doesn't tell you what she thinks or feels."

Interesting. "Show you anything?"

"Yeah, she's got a few piercings and tatts. If you ask, she'll show you. She's not shy, just . . . private."

We both watched her bump and grind on the dance floor

and saw when the young guy tried to run his hand up from her hip to her breast. We also saw when her hand covered his and she bent his finger back so far the kid's knees buckled.

Without looking at the kid, she stepped away and kept dancing.

"She's certainly not your type, dude."

My muscles tensed and I glared at the bartender. "What's that supposed to mean?"

"Hey, man, no insult intended." He held up his hands. "I just meant you usually have the perfect little prep chicks hanging off you. Mia might be more than even Nick at Night can handle."

"Don't bet on it," I muttered and headed for the dance floor.

Before I could reach it, a hand with red-tipped fingernails landed in the middle of my chest and the stacked blonde from the bar was standing in front of me.

"I know you," she said.

"No, I don't think we've met." I looked over her shoulder to see Mia still alone. Impatience crept up on me. She wouldn't be alone for long.

"You're Nick Jamison, from 'Nick at Night.'" She stepped closer, making it hard not to look down her dress. "I'm a fan."

No woman was a fan of mine. Some were tolerant, but generally I got hate mail from women with boyfriends who were fans of mine. I looked into the blonde's sharp green eyes and knew immediately what she was up to. After years of having people trying to beg, bribe, or bully me for a mention in my column, I recognized the signs easily.

I pasted a gentle smile on my face and tried to step around her. "Honey, whatever you want mentioned in my column, you can forget it."

She moved with me. "But I'd be willing to pay for the shout-

113

out. However you prefer." She trailed one of her claws across my jaw and I pulled my head back.

"It doesn't work that way. Besides, I quit today, so there is no more 'Nick at Night.'"

With that I stepped around her and made a beeline for Mia.

6

Mia

I felt the heat of his gaze on me. I was used to people watching me dance, and I didn't care. Caitlyn had gotten tired about an hour earlier and left, but that didn't stop me from staying to dance. I used the dance as a way to lose myself. Often the music and motion worked as my muse, and I left the club only to stay up and work on a new piece of jewelry all night.

But this time I felt that heated stare all the way down to my core. When I looked around the bar from under my hair, I'd spotted him at the bar: Mr. Hot Guy from the park.

No such thing as coincidence, Cait's voice whispered in my head.

My muse had disappeared and I closed my eyes to imagine him dancing with me. I remembered the way he'd felt beneath me, his body fitting perfectly between my legs, his muscled chest flexing beneath my hands, and his lips against mine. I wanted to feel it again. Wanted to taste his skin under my tongue, to feel the heat build until we both burned up.

When a warm body brushed against me, I imagined it was him. But the guy had been clumsy, and his hands hadn't made my skin tingle. Not the way it did now, as I watched him stalk toward me like a big cat hunting in the jungle.

A ripple of hunger went through me as I met his gaze. He was hunting, and I was in the mood to be caught.

"Hello again," he purred.

He stopped when there was just six inches between us. His hips rolled, and without a hitch, his body matched my rhythm. He didn't touch me, though. He was oh so close, yet not close enough.

"Hi, stranger," I replied, inching close enough to bump against him.

He put his hands on my hips and pulled me tight to him, his hard thigh thrusting between my legs. "You're not running away this time."

"I wasn't running last time."

He pressed his forehead against mine as our bodies moved in perfect tandem. "I'm Dominick," he said.

I licked my lips, tasting his breath on them. I slid my hands over his bulging biceps and clasped them around his neck. "I'm Mia."

Then I kissed him.

He tasted even better than I remembered. I nipped at his bottom lip, licked the corner of his mouth, and slid my lips teasingly against his until he growled. With one thrust of his tongue he took control of the kiss, taking it from teasing and seductive to hungry and animalistic.

Arousal flooded me hard and fast. My nipples hardened and my insides trembled with need. I pressed against him, grinding my hips against his erection and my breasts against his chest as my nails dug into his shoulders. Someone bumped against me and we both stumbled.

"Wait," I gasped, pulling away from him, "we can't do this."

He grabbed my hand and pulled me off the dance floor. He

waved to Jimmy and pushed through the staff door and down the back hallway. Did he work there? How could I have never noticed him before?

I was almost skipping to keep up with his long legs. Thank God I was used to dancing around in heels, or he'd have an accident on his hands instead of a semi turned-on woman. Okay, a very turned-on single woman who hadn't had sex in too long.

When we hit the parking, he spun me around quickly and trapped me against a sleek black Mustang. "Why not?"

His erection pressed against my sex and the rough denim of his jeans rubbed against my bare inner thighs, making it extremely hard to think. "I can't—I don't want to start anything."

My heart pounded and my hips flexed against him eagerly, but I kept my hands flat on the cool surface of the vehicle behind me. If I touched him again, I'd be lost.

"Honey, it's already started." His mouth came down on mine and I moaned.

I twisted and tore my mouth away, angling my face away from him. But he didn't give up. Instead, he nibbled his way across my jaw to my ear. He sucked on my earlobe and a shudder went through me. With a small moan I lifted a leg, wrapped it around his, and rubbed against him.

"I don't want a relationship," I panted. I had to be sure he knew that up front.

"Neither do I," he muttered against my neck.

"Just sex?" I mumbled.

"Just sex," he agreed before wrapping his hand in my hair and holding my head still for another knee-knocking kiss.

I reached around him and filled my hands with firm, round ass, pulling him closer. He rocked into me and I moaned. So good, he felt so good. But his jeans were in the way, the material too thick. I slid a hand between us and worked on his belt buckle. His hand fisted in my hair and a shiver ripped through me. I got his belt undone, then his button and zipper, and I slid my hand under the elastic of his shorts and grasped his hardness. Long and thick, he throbbed against the palm of my hand. I ran my thumb over the crown and he shuddered against me.

"Stop." He pulled away. He shifted me to the left and opened the door of the Mustang. "Get in."

Our eyes met and I couldn't stop the grin from creeping across my face. "This is going to be good," I said, and slid into the passenger seat.

Dominick dashed around the back of the car and got behind the wheel. He hadn't bothered to do up his pants and I couldn't resist. I reached out and cupped him through the cotton of his shorts. "My place is two blocks away."

We didn't speak as he drove. I kept my hand on his cock the whole time, stroking him, testing his size and sensitivity. His harsh breathing filled the interior of the car, but he kept both hands on the steering wheel. He was big, and harder than steel. It was all I could do not to climb on his lap while he drove.

The second he pulled up to the curb in front of my apartment and slid the car into park, he reached over and dragged me across his lap.

"You are such a tease," he growled.

"I'm not teasing. I'm horny."

We met in a heated, open-mouthed kiss. His hands slid under my thighs and helped me shift until I was straddling him. I balanced on my knees, my hands gripping his shoulders as he reached under the elastic of my thong and ran a finger along my slit.

He groaned. "You're so wet already."

"Now," I commanded, spreading my knees more and lowering myself against him so I could rock against his hard-on. "Fuck me now."

Dominick didn't hesitate, he shifted and shuffled, groaning as I nipped at his neck, then soothed it with a soft lick. "Move back," he urged, reaching between us.

I whimpered, not wanting to lose the incredible friction on my sex. When I realized he was trying to put a condom on, I backed off and slid a hand between my thighs. I shoved the thin material of my thong out of the way and rubbed at my rock-hard clit.

"God, you're sexy." Dominick lifted my skirt so he could see what I was doing. With a growl he gripped my hips and tugged me down, right onto his rigid cock.

"Yes!" I cried out. "Fuck, yes!" I ground down, rotating my hips as he stretched my insides. I'd never felt so full. If I hadn't been so goddamn horny, I'm sure he'd have ripped me in half. As it was, the pain was slight and made his invasion all the more pleasurable.

I gripped his shoulders, kept my forehead braced against his, and started to ride him. We locked gazes, both panting, his hands guiding my movements, and he thrust up to meet me. There was fire in his eyes. Fire that matched the flames licking at my insides. The rhythm of his harsh breathing matched mine, and I felt as if I was looking at my other half.

In that instant, his grip on me tightened, he swelled inside me and we both closed our eyes. I ground down and cried out as sparks went off inside me, showering pleasure through every fiber of my being.

Completely boneless, I curled up against Dominick, nuzzling my nose against his neck and breathing his spiced musk scent. Seconds, minutes, hours later for all I knew, I felt his chest start to shake beneath me.

"What?" I mumbled, still floating on a soft cloud of satisfaction.

"You are a wild cat," he said with a chuckle. One of his hands rubbed soothingly up and down my back; the other squeezed my bare butt cheek.

"Me?" I tried to infuse innocence into my voice, but instead I just sounded pleased. Hell, I was pleased.

"Yes, you." He pulled back and kissed my cheek. "You realize we're only twenty feet from the door? Yet here we sit like a couple of horny teenagers making out in a car."

"Hmmm. It was a first for me."

"Really?" The purr was back in his voice. "Maybe we should go inside and find out what other firsts I can help you with?"

7

Dominick

I couldn't believe it.

I watched the sway of Mia's skirt as she sauntered up the walk and unlocked her apartment building. She had great legs. A great walk, too. The way she walked was almost as sexy as the way she danced.

But it was nothing compared to the way she rode me.

I groaned and squeezed my eyes shut at the thought. We'd been in such a rush, we'd actually had sex in the car, *right in front of her door!*

How bad was that?

It's not that I'm against sex in public places. One particular lady friend, who I was still friends with, had been very into that sort of thing. When we'd been dating, I'd done my best to accommodate her kink. At the park, in the men's room at a nightclub, even a changing room at The Gap!

The fact that she'd been a cop had made it feel slightly safer and a bit more dangerous at the same time.

No, it wasn't that Mia had rocked my world in a public

place. It was the fact that it had been completely unplanned. I haven't lost control like that since . . . well, ever!

"Do you want a drink, Dominick?" she asked as soon as I closed the apartment door.

"No, I'm good, thanks."

"Oh, I know you're good. I was asking if you wanted a drink." She winked at me and my blood headed south again.

Jesus. I'd just come harder than I could ever remember and already I wanted her again.

Trying not to look like a complete horndog, I followed her into the living room. The big stereo system she had didn't surprise me; a woman who moved like she did probably danced naked around her apartment all the time.

Okay, so maybe that only happened in my dreams.

What did surprise me was the long wooden table set up along one wall with all sorts of tools and spools. Obviously, Mia wasn't your typical woman who needed to make every space into a dream home or something.

I walked over and fingered a soldering iron.

"What is it you do for a living, Mia?"

"I'm a jewelry designer."

She said it with such a sense of pride that I stopped examining the tools and looked back at her. Her cheeks were flushed and her eyes were glowing. "Jewelry?"

"Yeah, I work with silver and stuff. Come see."

She grabbed the sleeve of my shirt and pulled me behind her, down the short hallway and into a small bedroom. There was another worktable and then a shelf unit full of plastic containers. She pulled me over to the worktable, and on the end was a plastic tree thing with bright, sparkly silver earrings and stuff hanging from it.

Some of it was so amazingly delicate that I knew it wouldn't have been easy to make. She looked at me expectantly and I made what I hoped were appropriate sounds of approval. "Very nice. You made these?"

She folded her arms across her chest and raised a delicate eyebrow. "You don't like them."

"No, I think they're pretty." I just didn't know what the hell they were. They didn't look like any jewelry I'd ever seen before.

"You might have a better idea if you'd managed to actually fondle a breast while we were getting busy."

Ouch!

"Me? You were the one in such a hurry you were jerking me off while I drove. You practically jumped on my dick the second I turned the car off!" My blood heated to a boiling point and my idiot of a dick was standing at full attention, loving every minute of it.

"Well, I'm sorry," she snapped. "But it was your own fault. If you hadn't gotten me so goddamn worked up in the parking lot, I would've had more patience."

"Well, you weren't exactly Miss Demure back on that dance floor, were you?" I stepped close enough to feel the heat crackle between us. Her chest rose and fell rapidly, her nipples poking against her filmy little top, begging for me to touch. My hands itched with the knowledge that I still hadn't gotten to play with those luscious little tits yet. "After watching you dance like that, I couldn't think straight."

"Can you think straight now?" As if she'd read my mind, she whipped her shirt over her head and stood there like a goddess, daring me to touch her.

At the end of my leash, I reached out and palmed both of her breasts, pushing her back against the wall and smashing my mouth down on hers at the same time. She met fire with fire, kissing me back with more passion than I'd ever experienced. Her tongue rubbed against mine, her teeth nipped at my lips, and her hands tugged at my shirt, pulling it from my waistband.

She tore her mouth out from under me. "Off," she commanded.

I pulled back for a split second and she got rid of my shirt. Then we were skin against skin. God, she was so soft and supple. I kissed her ear, her neck. Squeezed her breasts. They were perfect, slightly bigger than a handful and firm, yet soft. Both nipples were hard and pointy, but one had a silver shank through it. A barbell that made me want to be gentle. I cradled her breast in my hand and licked it gently. Then I flicked my tongue at it and she moaned.

I rolled the other nipple between thumb and forefinger, tugging on it and feeling her body writhe against mine. Her nails scraped up my back and into my hair, where she pressed against me. I got the hint and opened my mouth over her pierced nipple.

I tongued the barbell, then sucked. Her back arched and she cried out.

God, she was sensitive. I switched breasts, using my teeth to gently worry the other one while I reached under her skirt and pulled the scrap of panties away. She kicked them away and hooked a leg over my hip, grinding against my hard-on.

Slipping a hand between us, I groaned when I felt her wetness. She was so slick and hot. My cock throbbed and jumped in my pants, eager to get inside that warmth. But I wasn't going to let that happen again. I was not going to be the two-minute wonder again. Instead, I slid two fingers inside her and started pumping, using the heel of my hand against the hard nub of her clit. She arched and writhed some more, her cunt tightening around my fingers. I bit her nipple gently and she cried out again. "Yes, now, don't stop."

I switched breasts, taking the pierced one in my mouth again as I fucked her with my fingers. Scraping my teeth across her extrasensitive nipple, I curled my fingers and felt her begin to tremble.

"That's it, baby," I crooned against her soft skin. "Come for me."

I pinned her to the wall with my body and bit down on her nipple. "Yes!" she screamed, every muscle in her body tensing as fluid soaked my hand and she came. Hard.

8

Dominick

Once Mia stopped quaking in my arms, I lifted her against my chest and stepped into the hallway.

"Bedroom?" I asked.

She lifted a limp hand and pointed to the other closed door. Duh! If I'd taken another step I'd have seen the third room was the bathroom. Not caring that I might've looked like an idiot, I pushed the second door open and strode to the bed.

I dropped her onto the mattress and made quick work of getting out of my jeans. And my socks. I knew enough about women to realize that leaving them on, no matter how much of a hurry I was in or how good her orgasm had just been, was a mistake.

When I straightened, she lay there, eyes slitted, the fingers of one hand trailing over her own breast. She bent her legs, planted her feet on the mattress, and spread her knees, giving a perfect view of her pretty pink pussy.

"Your turn," she purred.

I slid a condom on with trembling fingers before climbing between her legs. I slid my cock over her slit, just enjoying the feel of her lying there, waiting for me. Poised at her entrance, I looked into her eyes and felt a connection snap into place. My heart swelled as I slid into her body.

Such a perfect fit. Tight, hot, wet, and completely magical.

Light danced behind her dark eyes as she wrapped her arms around my shoulders and I started to move. I tried to go slow. I'd started off slow, but soon my hips were pumping in and out, the friction delicious as Mia curled her body up and wedged her knees under my shoulders. Deep . . . so deep, and hot. My balls slapped against her ass as we both panted. Our eyes were locked as my heart pounded. Something was happening here.

Something way out of my league.

"Come on, baby. It's your turn to come for me. Come in me." Her hands slid over my hips and she cupped my ass and I groaned. She felt so good I didn't want to come. I didn't want to stop. My body wasn't listening to me, though. Pressure built rapidly at the base of my cock. My head got light, my dick throbbed and pulsed, her nails bit into my backside, and that was it.

I almost blacked out from the pleasure before I collapsed on top of Mia, shifting to the side slightly, but still holding on to her as I fought for breath.

The mattress was soft beneath me, and Mia was warm and pliant. With her in my arms, my body spent and my heartbeat starting to steady . . . everything felt different. There was no pressing need deep inside to hurry up and get out.

When I felt steady enough, I stood and left the room. I got rid of the condom in the garbage can next to the toilet and turned the cold water up full. After splashing my face several times, I eyed the reflection staring back at me in the mirror.

The man in the mirror looked shaken. Like things would never be the same.

Closing my eyes, I took a deep breath and turned my brain off. After drying my face and hands with the hanging towel, I went and crawled back into bed. Mia was already under the covers, and when I stretched out on my back, she curled against my side without a word and I wrapped an arm around her.

9

Mia

"So tell me again what this is?"

Dominick's eyes sparkled as he held up a delicate silver chain and the thin ring of surgical steel attached to it.

"It's a waist chain, and this"—I held up the little hoop—"is for a clitoral piercing."

"Clitoral?"

I swallowed a giggle as Dominick worked the idea around in his mind. For a guy who was such a player, he was sort of innocent. It appealed to the devil inside me.

And he was a player. Or I should say, he used to be.

I'd learned that the first week we'd been seeing each other. Dominick Jamison used to be "Nick at Night." Sort of a male version of Carrie Bradshaw from *Sex and the City*. He was good-looking, charming, and had all the right moves in a bed, and out of it.

But every now and then, I could shake him up . . . and I loved it.

When frustration had finally knocked me on my ass this morning with another rejection from yet another retailer, instead of going to Caitlyn for a massage like I normally would, I'd dialed Dominick and greeted him at the door naked. And he'd done his best to put a smile on my face again. The teasing rapport that was natural between us was almost as good as the sex.

"What's wrong, Mr. Man's Man? You mean to tell me you've never seen a woman with a pierced pinky?"

"Pinky?" His lips twitched.

"What? I can't be discreet with my wording?"

He waggled his eyebrows. "You weren't being discreet with your wording an hour ago."

"That's not a very gentlemanly thing to say to a lady." I straightened my posture and primly laid a piece of paper towel across my lap. After a bout of energetic bedroom gymnastics, we were at my kitchen table eating fried egg sandwiches that *he* made while I sat at the table and pouted over my homeless jewelry.

"You're right." He inclined his head. "I'm sorry. We're not in the bedroom, so I'll let you be a lady."

He winked at me as he took a bite out of his sandwich and I set aside my jewelry to dig into my own.

He was the perfect part-time lover. Except for the fact that I was starting to care about that lost look that crept into his eyes whenever he talked about writing.

We ate in comfortable silence—him glancing occasionally at the jewelry, then at me. "Thanks for coming over," I said when I was done eating my sandwich.

"Glad I could be of service."

"What were you up to?"

"Working on an article for a men's health magazine."

"Yeah?" I got up and put our plates in the sink, refilled our coffee mugs, and sat down again. "What's it about?"

I swear he blushed.

"Dominick? What's it about?"

"It's a fluff piece on how to impress a woman on a first date."

A slight pang went through me. "I suppose you're pretty good at that, huh?"

He shrugged. "It doesn't take much to know that everyone likes to feel like they're attractive and sexy. It's just that some guys don't know how to make a woman feel that way."

Ignoring the fact that we'd never been on a first date, I tucked a foot underneath my butt and gave him a long look.

"Is this really what you want to do?"

"What do you mean?" He shifted back in his chair, crossing his arms in front of him.

"I mean, do you want to write freelance articles on how to impress women forever?"

"Sure, why not? Most men would kill to be able to make a living writing fluff."

Should I or shouldn't I?

We'd agreed that first night together that we were both in this *relationship* only for the sex. So really I had no right to probe too closely, but I couldn't help it. I hadn't known that first night that two weeks later he'd be sitting in my kitchen after making me a fried egg sandwich for lunch.

I took a deep breath. "As charming as you can be, I don't think writing fluff pieces is the right career for you."

He stiffened. "You think you know me so well?"

"I think I know you well enough."

He snorted. "What do you know that makes you think this is so wrong for me?"

"If you enjoyed writing puff pieces, you wouldn't have quit *The City* paper over a false recommendation."

"There was more to it than that."

"Like what?"

He glared.

"Glare all you want. You don't scare me." We'd argued enough that I knew when he was seriously mad. I also knew I was pushing it, but I couldn't shake the feeling that he was hiding something. Maybe even hiding it from himself.

I got up from my seat and went to his side of the table. Swinging a leg over him, I straddled his lap and clasped his face in my hands. "Tell me what you really want to do, Dominick."

"I don't know what you mean."

God, he was stubborn!

"You do know what I mean. Tell me what it is that's in here." I placed a hand on his bare chest. "What it is you want to do but are afraid to try."

"I'm not afraid," he snapped. "I'm just not ready yet."

"Ready for what?"

"To write a novel," he muttered, avoiding my eyes.

"That's a great idea! What kind of novel?"

"A thriller."

"Tell me more."

So he did. I sat on his lap and watched him come alive in a way I'd only seen when we were making love. And it hit me: I was falling in love with him. Shit, I was past falling, I *was* in love with him.

"But that's something I'll do in a couple of years. I'm not ready yet."

Dominick looked at me expectantly.

Oh yeah, the book. "You know, I think you should do it now. What better time? You just quit your job. You said yourself you have savings that will last you a while, so you don't really *need* the freelance work. It's the perfect time."

He shook his head. "Nah, it's a dream, not work."

"What good is a dream if you don't go after it?"

He met my gaze and I saw the desire there. Not for me, but

for the dream. He really wanted to do it; he just needed a push. "Unless you really are too scared?"

His eyes narrowed, and before I knew what he was going to do, he kissed me.

Willing to stop thinking, I kissed him back and soon I was flat on my back on the table with my pants around my ankles.

"So lovely," he whispered, and nipped at my inner thigh. He used his thumbs to spread my swollen pussy lips before he blew softly across my sex.

"Don't tease me, Dominick," I begged. I spread my legs as wide as I could and lifted my hips off the table. "Please."

"Only because you said please."

He leaned in and wiggled his tongue between my slick folds. Then he swiped it the length of my sex, all the way to my clit. I gasped and pressed against him, and he took it in his mouth.

He suckled and flicked it with his tongue. He scraped it lightly with his teeth, then soothed it with a gentle kiss. I arched against him, sighs and whimpers escaping from me at an embarrassing rate.

Then he slipped a finger inside me and trailed another over my puckered rear entrance. Shock waves went through me and my insides clenched as my orgasm hit.

When I opened my eyes again, Dominick was standing at the edge of the table with a very pleased look on his face and I couldn't remember what we'd been talking about.

10

Dominick

I closed the file on "How to Impress on a First Date" for the last time and heaved a sigh. It had been hard to write. Not hard as in, I didn't know what I was doing. But hard as in, grueling, tedious torture. It had been boring to write.

Ignoring the e-mail from another editor, I got up from the computer and went to the kitchen. I pulled a frozen pizza out and slid it into the oven, then wandered around the apartment. It was more than the article being boring . . . I was bored.

If I really thought about it, I'd been bored for a long time, even with the column. That was why it had started to grate on my nerves so bad when people called me Nick instead of Dom or Dominick.

I didn't know exactly when it happened, but I wasn't that guy anymore. I hadn't enjoyed going out and about town in . . . well, at least six months. Maybe even a year. Being the "man about town" had stopped being fun and had just been my job, and a habit.

Another thing I'd noticed over the last months was that people who I thought were friends didn't really know me, or care. In the two weeks since I'd quit, my phone and e-mail messages had dropped dramatically, and the silence was very telling.

The timer on the oven went off and I pulled out the pizza. I grabbed a beer from the fridge and went to sit on the patio and eat. The time had come to figure out what I really wanted to do.

Ah, hell. I knew what it was. Damn Mia for bringing that desire to the forefront of my brain. I wanted to be an author. Not just a writer, but an author. I wanted to tell stories that would entertain millions, not just the singles of the city. I was tired of the connections game, of the "who's good enough to be given a shout-out in my column."

I just wanted to write, to tell a good story. And I knew just the one. It had been simmering in the back of my mind for years, just waiting for me to plant my ass in the chair and go for it.

Without giving myself a chance to think about it again, I jumped to my feet and went back inside. I set my plate in the sink and exchanged my empty beer for a fresh cold one before returning to my computer. I opened a new file and started typing.

Cutler knew the minute the call came over the radio it was going to be a rough night. His gut clenched and the hair on the back of his neck stood up in warning. It had started again.

Doing my best to hold on to my anger so I wouldn't feel the hurt buried beneath it, I yanked open the door to Vesna's Retreat and stormed in. How my aunt still had the power to hurt me I'll never know.

"Caitlyn's with a client," Vesna said from behind the juice bar.

I plopped my butt down on a barstool. "I'll wait."

Vesna smiled and kept unpacking a box of what looked like essential oils. "Your chi is unbalanced, Mia."

"Yeah? Well, my life is unbalanced, so that's no surprise."

She didn't speak again. A minute later, I reached out. "I'm sorry, Vesna. I didn't mean to snap at you."

"It's okay." The older woman smiled gently. "Your display is dangerously empty."

I glanced at the corner where my jewelry display was set up. She was right! There was only one pair of earrings and two navel rings left!

"You sold all that?" My pulse was racing. I worried that she was pulling my leg, that the display had fallen over or something and she had the stock behind the counter.

"Yes, it is sold. I'll write you a check."

Yay! It sold. Someone—several someones actually—bought my jewelry from a store! Well, not a store, but the clinic. Whatever. Either way, it was a step up from going to craft sales. It was almost professional!

"Will you bring more in?" Vesna asked as she held out a check to me.

More?

"Of course." I took another look at the display. It had only held earrings and navel studs. "Do you think you'd be willing to carry some of the other products since they're doing so well?"

My fingers itched as I held the check in my lap. I wanted desperately to look at the sum, but I didn't want to appear too eager or unprofessional in front of the chic businesswoman.

"I don't want any of those . . ." She waved her hands around her groin area.

"What about nipple rings? I have some lovely ones with small gemstones in them. Silver and gold." I didn't have any gold ones, but I could make up a couple over the weekend. "When on display they don't look any more risqué than the belly button ones."

I watched, body tensed as she thought about it.

"Hmmm." She shook her head. "I cannot say for sure without seeing them. You can bring them in to show me first?"

The urge to lift up my shirt and show her the one in my own nipple was strong, but I fought it off.

"Yes," I nodded, "I'll bring some in when I restock on Monday?"

It was Wednesday, so that gave me a few days to work with the gold I'd picked up last week. Vesna agreed to a Monday afternoon appointment and went back to her oils. I took the first chance to peek at the check still clutched in my fingers.

Almost four hundred dollars!

"Mia! What's up sister?"

My head snapped up at Caitlyn's words and I watched as she entered the reception area from the back. "I see you got your check."

I grinned at her. Then a thought occurred to me. "You didn't buy any of it, did you? Because if you did, I'm going to have to kick your ass."

A tsking sound from Vesna reminded me that we weren't alone. Vesna was a sweetheart, or so Caitlyn said—I didn't know her well enough to have an opinion—but she had certain ideas of how ladies behaved. And cursing was frowned on.

"Oops," I mouthed to Cait.

"Vesna, Janie is my last appointment of the day. Is it okay if I leave a few minutes early?"

Vesna glanced from Caitlyn to me and smiled. "You girls go have some fun."

"She called you a slut? What a bitch!"

I nodded in total agreement with my friend. We were at Bright Lights, the bar where we often hung out and danced. Also the one where I'd run into Dominick that first night. Not wanting to think about Dominick, I concentrated on the conversation at hand and what had pissed me off so much earlier.

"Another margarita, Jimmy?"

The bartender nodded at us and stopped cutting limes to make us a couple of drinks. It was early still, only just after eight, and the bar was empty. Caitlyn and I liked it this way because we could talk, and Jimmy was always quick to get our refills. When it got busy later, we'd hit the dance floor.

"She didn't out and out call me a slut." A sense of fairness

141

made me make that clear. "That would be too crass for her. What she actually said was they didn't expect me to bring a date. At first I thought it was because she didn't think I could get one, because that's her usual thing. But then she commented about how she knew it was hard for me to keep a steady boyfriend with my *lifestyle*." I screwed up my face and mimicked her, "*'It's not an insult, dear, I know you're just . . . relaxed in your relationships.'*"

Caitlyn choked on the sip she'd just taken from her fresh drink. "So what are you going to do?"

"I don't know. I mean, it's my uncle's sixtieth birthday and I want to go. I'm just not sure I can deal with my aunt and cousin without ruining the dinner. But I can't tell if she thinks I'm a slut or an old maid. I just don't think I'm in the mood to deal with them."

"Well, since Aunt Bea was such a treat when she invited you, I'm sure she wouldn't be surprised if you didn't show."

"I know."

I stared into my glass for a few minutes. It was times like these that I really missed my parents. I felt so . . . lost. All I'd ever wanted was to belong and be accepted, but my family just didn't have it in them to even try to look beneath the surface. Normally when I was around them, I threw my individualism in their face as a result. Wearing the most gaudy nose ring or showing off a new tattoo.

It had been clear when Aunt Bea had called earlier to remind me about my uncle's birthday that she thought I was a complete flake. Worse, a single and unemployed flake. Or a complete skank.

So what if I was single, sort of? Or unemployed, sort of? They just didn't get me, and I was tired of trying to explain.

As if she'd read my thoughts, Caitlyn turned to me. "What

about Dominick? You could ask him to go to the dinner with you. That should shut her up somewhat."

"I don't know if that's a good idea." I shrugged.

"Why not? You're still dating him, right?"

"Dating isn't exactly the term I'd use. 'Seeing him' might work." I'd definitely seen all of him, and the remembered yummy-ness was making my pulse pick up, even now. "Except I haven't seen him in almost a week."

"A week isn't long," Caitlyn said.

It wasn't, either. Especially considering we weren't really a couple. It was just supposed to be a sex thing.

"I think I might've crossed the line the last time I saw him."

"What'd you do?" She smirked at me and I sighed.

"I didn't *do* anything. Not really."

She gazed at me steadily and I felt a twinge in my belly. "Okay, so I sort of told him he was scared to follow his dreams."

Caitlyn laughed and shook her head. "Mia, one of these days you're going to dare the wrong person to do something and it's gonna bite you on your butt."

"I think it just did." I actually missed Dominick. His sarcasm, his laughter . . . his passion. I even missed arguing with him.

Pretty sad considering we'd never even been on a date.

12

Mia

No guts, no glory.

God, why did I take stupid little sayings like that as gospel? The doorbell buzzer sounded and I tore my gaze away from the mirror. This was going to be fun.

Not.

I shuffled down the hallway and reached for the door.

"Wow!" Dominick said when he saw me.

I could've said the same thing. He looked damn good. Black button-up shirt undone at the collar—I could see just enough of his curly hair there to make my palms itch—tucked into crisp, pressed trousers that were just a bit snug in all the right places.

Saliva pooled in my mouth. He looked downright edible. And I looked . . . "Bad?"

His eyes ran over me, and when they met mine they had that special gleam in them. "Not bad, just different."

"Shit."

I headed straight back to bathroom at the end of the short hallway and stared in the mirror. I didn't look like my normal self. And it was more than the lack of heavy eyeliner or fire engine red lipstick.

I'd pinned my hair up in a twist, but the streaks were still there. Maybe I should leave it down. I didn't want to go too far and have them know I'd tried so hard. But I really wanted the dinner to go smoothly. My uncle was the most tolerant of them all, and I think he actually loved me. He was just too much into his own world to notice how much of a bitch his wife and daughter were.

"You look beautiful, Mia," Dom said from his position perched against the doorjamb.

"I don't look like me." I frowned, unable to decide why I cared what I looked like. Only my family could make me so neurotic.

"I can fix that for you."

My heart jumped as I watched Dominick in the mirror. He stepped into the bathroom and pressed against my back. His lips pressed against my neck, his hands went around my waist, and I felt his cock swell against my ass. "All that's missing is that wicked glow of a satisfied woman."

A sigh floated from my lips as his hand slid under my blouse and cupped a breast. After a quick squeeze he moved the lace cup down and tugged on the ring there.

"You changed your piercing," he murmured.

I closed my eyes, nodding as I pressed back against him.

"No," he said. "Open your eyes. Watch in the mirror."

I reached back and tried to pull him into me further, but instead he backed away. He met my gaze in the mirror.

"Hands on the counter," he commanded. "Bend forward for me and we won't even mess you up."

Already breathing hard, I leaned forward and gripped the edges of the counter. I arched my back and widened my stance, sticking my ass out rudely.

"Oh, yes," Dominick sighed. He ran his hands over my hips and down my thighs before lifting my skirt and chuckling. "A little bit of innocence and a whole lot of naughty. I love it."

He fingered the back of my white lace thong, following it down between my cheeks to my pouting pussy.

"Dominick," I growled. I knew he loved to tease, oh how he loved to tease, but I couldn't handle it. We hadn't been together in over a week and my body was more than ready for him. I was more than ready for this.

He read the warning in my eyes and I heard the clink of his belt buckle and the rasp of a metal zipper. "Okay?" The head of his cock nudged at my entrance.

"Oh, yes," I sighed, and pushed back at the same time he surged forward, filling me up.

I watched in the mirror as his forehead puckered and his cheeks flushed. I locked my knees and stood still as he slid in and out of me, the slow, delicious friction making my insides tremble.

He leaned over me, cupping my breast and toying with the ring as he nipped at my neck. "That's it," I cried out as I felt him swell and throb deep within me.

My insides tightened and my heart raced. I was on the edge, pleasure building until I was ready to burst. But the burst wasn't coming. My eyes pleaded with him in the mirror and his other hand dropped between my thighs as he pumped faster and harder. He circled my clit, and the pressure built some more. But I couldn't get over the edge; I was strung too tight.

"Argghh!" I cried out, frustrated.

His arms tightened around me and he groaned as his own orgasm hit and warmth flooded my insides.

Dominick rested his chin on my shoulder and met my gaze in the mirror. "I'm sorry. You just felt so damn good and I couldn't wait any longer."

I smiled, not upset that I hadn't come. Strange, but watching him come had almost been as good.

"It's okay, babe; you can make it up to me after dinner." If he was still talking to me after he listened to my family trot out all my bad qualities. "Besides, if you'd waited for me, you might never get to come."

He kissed my cheek and pulled out. "Don't move," he warned.

My head fell forward and I relaxed my neck, staying where I was as he ran the taps and used a warm, damp cloth to clean me up. My heart pounded as he adjusted my thong again and pulled my skirt down. He pulled me up straight and fixed my bra, after placing a soft kiss on each nipple through the material of my shirt.

"We didn't use a condom," he said softly.

"I know."

"I'm safe. I'd never do anything to hurt you."

"Same here."

I gazed into his eyes and saw such tenderness and affection there that my breath caught in my throat.

Neither of us was ready for more words, but sometimes words aren't needed. First, no condom, then the simple task of him putting me back together so carefully . . . There was true intimacy there. Not just physical, and we both knew it.

"Now you look like you," he whispered.

My brow furrowed. "I look the same."

He brushed a thumb across my cheek. "No, now your sparkle is back. We can't let them take away your sparkle."

13

Dominick

I tried not to stare, but I was having a hard time concentrating on driving with Mia tense as a ticking time bomb next to me. I knew when she'd called yesterday that the dinner tonight was important to her just by the quaver in her voice, but I hadn't realized just how important.

As soon as I'd said yes to her, she'd ended the conversation, and I hadn't been able to ask. But I'd realized a couple of things.

One: A week had gone by without seeing her, but the sound of her voice on the phone had brought such an intense rush of pleasure that my chest had hurt.

Two: We'd never been on a real date before.

My night had been shot as far as work went after that. It had been all I could do not to call her up and ask if I could go over then and there.

Then the third realization hit: Not only did I want to see her, I wanted to be with her. Even if it was just cuddling on the sofa watching a movie. In fact, the cuddling thing had sounded really good.

I also wanted to print out some of the pages of my novel and have her read them. I'd been writing nonstop and had just over 150 pages. It seems once I decided to open the door to Byron Cutter, the guy wouldn't rest until his story was told.

It had been like he was living inside my head, taking over my life, until I'd heard Mia's voice again.

I parked the car and turned off the engine. Turning to her, I reached for her hand and cradled it between mine. Her hand was clammy and she was so quiet. "Before we go in there, you want to tell me why a family get-together has you so tense?"

She shrugged. "My family is a bit different than I am."

"How different?"

She met my gaze. "They're normal."

I laughed. "You're normal, darling."

She shook her head. "Not to them I'm not."

"What?" I didn't get it. Family was family. Normal was relative.

Of course, my parents were free-loving hippies who didn't believe in marriage despite the fact that they'd been together monogamously for more than forty years, and my sister ran the country's first art gallery that focused only on erotic art.

An idea hit me right between those ideas and I opened my mouth to speak, but Mia tugged at my hand, and said, "Let's go in before I lose my nerve."

Mia, the woman who had kissed me senseless in the park, then flipped off a stranger, lose her nerve? Now I was worried.

14

Mia

I almost felt sorry for Dominick as we entered the restaurant. I knew what was coming and I wanted to warn him, but what could I say? *Hey, be prepared to be treated like a leper?*

The hostess greeted Dominick by name. Or should I say she greeted him as Nick. After trading basic pleasantries, he said we were there to meet the Jones party and she gave me a once-over. And surprisingly, she smiled.

That made me feel a little better about my appearance. Normally, snotty blond hostesses looked down on my funky style, and I'd expected nothing less in the best five-star restaurant in town. Of course, I was as plain as I could ever be with the gray rayon top and knee-length black skirt. I even wore clear nail polish and pumps, not boots.

As we were led to the table, I noticed that everyone around us was dressed a lot nicer. Fancy, sparkly dresses for the ladies and the men in suits. I looked at Dominick in his casual shirt and trousers and felt okay with him next to me. No one would even notice me if he kept on smiling.

When we got to the table, my Uncle Ron stood and I hugged him. "Happy Birthday," I whispered in his ear.

Uncle Ron was basically a good guy. I think he learned long ago how to tune out the world around him as a safety mechanism so he didn't go crazy. And while I could understand his need to do that, part of me would always resent that he hadn't somehow taught me how to do that, too. If he had, it would've made my teenage years a lot more bearable.

Hell, it would've made the thought of this dinner a lot more bearable.

"This is Dominick Jamison, everyone. Dominick, this is Ron and Beatrice Jones, and my cousin, Sharon." I glanced at the other man at the table and waited for someone to introduce us, but the silence lengthened.

"I'm Mia, and this is Dominick." I reached across the table and shook his hand.

"Oh, I'm sorry, Mia, I didn't realize you hadn't met Ashton yet. We've been seeing each other for almost six months, you know?" Sharon's perfect smile didn't quite reach her eyes when she spoke.

Dominick held my chair out and we sat down. The waitress, bless her heart, was there immediately. "I'll have a tequila and soda, please."

"Mia dear, tequila isn't a proper drink to have with dinner. Why don't you have some white wine, or just soda?"

I smiled at the waitress. "Tequila, please."

Aunt Bea's lips pursed, but she didn't say anything else, and I was grateful when Dominick put his hand on my thigh under the table. He ordered a beer and then turned to the group. "You've chosen a great place for a birthday dinner. Have you eaten here before?"

"You've eaten here before?" Sharon's surprise was clear on her pinched face.

"It's been a while, but I used to eat here quite regularly. The grilled salmon is top-notch, but I have to say the prime rib is my favorite."

Uncle Ron jumped on the topic of dinner and I listened as the men talked about different steak cuts and meat. Who knew Dominick was so good at dinner conversation? Literally.

"He's quite a catch. How did you manage that?"

I turned to Sharon, but before I could answer, Dominick did, "She jumped on me in the park one day and kissed me. I was hooked after that."

"Mia!" Aunt Bea gasped.

Sharon scowled.

Ashton chuckled and looked at me with an almost lascivious gleam in his eyes.

Uncle Ron had his head buried in the menu, completely oblivious.

I looked at Dominick, shocked.

"Was that yesterday or earlier today?" Sharon had obviously gotten her bearings back.

"No, it was just over a month ago. I've been chasing her ever since. I'm hoping one day she'll let me catch her." He winked at me and took a long pull from his beer.

That was the end of *that* conversation. I knew Bea and Sharon were both dying to grill him, but propriety kept them quiet. That was, until dinner was served and the chef came out of the kitchen to check on us.

"Dominick! It's been too long, bro."

Dominick stood up and shook hands with the lanky blonde. "Sorry, Ray, things have changed a little for me lately. But I admit, I've missed your cooking."

Ray was a good-looking guy. Young, too, for a chef, but good-looking in a rough way that even clean-shaven and dressed in kitchen whites couldn't hide.

"Yeah, I saw your final column. I thought for sure I'd see or hear from you after that. What happened, man?"

He glanced meaningfully at me. "I got a little distracted."

Dominick introduced me to the chef *as his girlfriend*, then told him we were there celebrating my uncle's sixtieth birthday.

"Your meal is on me, then, Mr. Jones. Happy birthday."

When Ray reached out to shake hands with my uncle, the sleeve of his pristine white coat lifted and his tattoos flashed.

"I gotta get back to the kitchen, Dom. But we need to get together soon, okay?"

"Definitely." Dominick nodded and waved him off. "Go do some work."

"That was Chef Raymond Labreque?" Aunt Bea stared at Dominick in amazement.

"That's him."

"Your column? You're 'Nick at Night,' aren't you?" This time the gleam in Ashton's eyes was almost greedy. "I know you."

Dominick's smile became less real as he shook his head. "I used to be 'Nick at Night.' I quit a while ago. The day I met Mia, actually."

"Who's 'Nick at Night'?" Sharon asked.

Ashton put his hand over hers on the table. "A newspaper columnist, dear. A 'man about town' sort of thing. A bit of a local celebrity among the men in this city."

"Hardly a celebrity," Dominick said.

"Nonsense." Ashton waved his hand airily. "In fact, I tried to get you to come into my shop a couple of months ago. Your editor assured me you would, but you never showed up. Too bad too, because it would've done wonders to have you mention my business in your column. I run a men's clothier's shop. Very high-end and expensive suits. Maybe you'd be interested in doing a promotional spot for me? A radio or even television ad?"

I could see the muscle in Dominick's jaw working overtime, and I reached under the table to put my hand on his thigh this time. I gave him a squeeze and looked Ashton in the eye.

"I do believe that shout-outs by 'Nick' could never be bought, they were only earned, and since he's already said he doesn't do that anymore, it's safe to say you missed your chance."

"Mia!"

"What?" I gave Sharon my best innocent look.

"So what do you do now that you've quit your column, Nick?"

I was past the point of embarrassment. My blood heated and a minute trembling started in my muscles.

"Why don't you just come right out and ask him if he's unemployed, Aunt Bea? That's what you want to know, right?" I stood up and tossed my napkin on the table. "I thought you guys would stick with being rude to me, I never for one minute thought you'd be so awful to a man you just met. A *guest* at dinner. We're leaving."

I reached into my purse and put a small jewelry box in front of my befuddled uncle. "Happy birthday. I made this just for you."

15

Mia

I could've cried I was so mad.

Dominick kept his hand on the small of my back as we left the restaurant, but he didn't speak. It was as if he knew I was just barely holding on to my temper.

"I'm sorry," I finally whispered once we were in the car and almost home.

"Hey," he said softly. "You don't have anything to be sorry for. In fact, it was sort of nice to hear the real Mia come to the fore. I was starting to get worried that your family had buried her somehow."

I stared out the window at the passing scenery. Dom had taken the long way home and we were driving through the river valley. It was nice, almost peaceful. The river, the trees, very little traffic.

"My parents were killed in a car accident when I was nine. Aunt Bea is my mom's sister, but I don't remember ever meeting them until I went to live with them."

Without looking at him, I spilled my guts. I told him how

I'd never felt like a part of the family. How my aunt's rigidity and my cousin's constant sniping had only encouraged me to dye my hair blue when I was fourteen and stay out all night when I was sixteen. I pierced my nose and got a tattoo to prove to them I was my own person and didn't need their approval.

"I was seventeen when I graduated high school and moved out. I didn't go to college, and I might only have been a secretary, but I've been supporting myself since then. I've never had to ask them for anything." I glanced over at Dominick with a sense of pride. "Sharon still lives with my aunt and uncle."

Dominick pulled up in front of my apartment and turned off the car. Yet, neither of us made a move to leave the cozy confines.

"I can't imagine living with people who don't allow you to be you," Dominick said softly. "My parents were just the opposite. Hippies in every sense of the word. They smoked pot and gave me and my sister the sex talk when we were ten." He chuckled. "I think they were actually disappointed I turned something so tame as a weekly column into a career."

I met his gaze. "But you've never doubted that they loved you."

He shook his head. "No, I never doubted it."

I swallowed and gave him a small smile. "I bet that article on how to impress on a first date is a real winner. You were my knight in shining armor tonight."

He threw back his head and laughed. "Some knight when you end up defending me before walking out without giving me a chance to stand up for you."

"I can stand up for myself. It was just nice not to have to do it alone this time." I leaned over and placed a gentle kiss on his lips. "Are you coming in?"

* * *

When we got into the apartment, there was no mad rush to get naked. Instead, Dominick flopped onto the sofa and patted the cushion beside him. "Let's just relax for a bit."

He turned on the television and flipped through the channels while I kicked off my shoes and curled up against his side.

He found a movie and I pretended to watch it with him while thoughts about the way things had gone swirled through my head. My "just sex" relationship with Dominick had become so much more. I was starting to care too much.

The biggest clue that he'd become more than just a lover was when I'd felt the urge to push him to go after his dreams. Why would I care if he chased his dreams if he was only my bed partner?

I'd missed him that past week. I thought I might've scared him away, but he'd been almost eager when I'd called, and he'd certainly been a wonderful date. It didn't matter if most people's dates didn't start with sex in front of the bathroom mirror. I wasn't most people, and Dominick wasn't either.

I couldn't believe I'd actually taken him to meet my family. And he hadn't run screaming for the hills afterward. Curled tight against his side on the sofa, with his arm wrapped around me, I felt safe and accepted as I drifted off to sleep.

16

Dominick

I should probably put Mia to bed and leave. It would be the gentlemanly thing to do; after all, this was our first real date. Only I didn't care if it was our first or our fiftieth, I didn't want to leave her.

After picking her up, I went down the short hallway to the bedroom and settled her on the middle of the bed. With slow, gentle movements I removed her clothes, noticing again the butterfly tattoos—one on the outside curve of her breast, the other larger one on the inside curve of her hip. She was like those tattoos: hidden to everyone except those she chose to trust.

Sure you could see butterflies, but not many people got to touch one.

Touch . . . I resisted the urge to play with the jeweled silver ring hanging from one nipple and wondered, not for the first time, why only one nipple? Why hadn't she pierced them both?

When she wore only her panties, the thought of leaving occurred again, maybe do the knight in shining armor thing, but then I thought of her waking up alone. After what she'd said, and meeting her family, I just couldn't do it. She'd had a rough night, and I wanted to make sure tomorrow was a better day for her.

So, I stripped down and climbed into bed next to her. *It's not like I've never spent the night before.*

I reached out and placed a hand on her soft belly, and sighed when she curled into me automatically. The heaviness in my chest lifted and I knew I was a goner. For once in my life, a woman felt completely right in my arms.

I tightened my hold. She belonged there.

I was dreaming.

Flat on my back in the park again with Mia straddling my lap. She was kissing me, whispering to me as she dragged her lips across my chin and down my neck.

Her hands trailed over my chest, leaving a wake of fire everywhere she touched as she toyed with my nipples until they were rock hard and I moaned her name. She kissed her way lower, her tongue dipping into my belly button, her teeth nipping at my inner thigh while her hair trailed over my hard-on.

We were naked in the park, the sunshine glorious on my skin, her light giggles music to my ears as she teased and teased until I arched my hips and said please.

Only then did she wrap her lips around my cock and suck gently. One hand circled the shaft, the other cupped my balls, rolling them between her fingers as she loved me with her mouth.

Her head rose and fell, her lips staying tight to me as her tongue pressed against the underside. The pressure built at the base; then she circled the sensitive head and everything inside me tightened. All feelings and sensations centered on my cock as she picked up speed, sucking a bit harder, her fingers gripping a bit tighter.

"Mia, please," I begged. My hands wrapped in her hair and I held her close as my hips lifted and I came hard.

Pulse pounding, body throbbing, everything I had left my body for her, only to come back in a wash of sensations that left me breathless and panting.

The ground shifted under me and Mia crawled back up my body and cuddled against me. "Thank you for staying last night."

17

Mia

Dominick was still asleep. I wasn't even sure he woke up when I'd loved him. It didn't really matter. Even in sleep it was my name he'd called out.

When did he become so dear to me?

His dark head rested starkly on my pillow and a fist tightened around my heart. I wanted it to be his pillow. I wanted to always be able to reach out in the night and find him.

I'd been on my own for so long. The yearning for a family, for camaraderie and love and open acceptance was buried deep. I had Caitlyn, my friend since eighth grade, my spirit sister. But that was it. It hadn't ever really bothered me, though. Having one person who loved and accepted me was more than a lot of people had. But now, looking at Dominick and remembering the way he'd been there for me the day before, I wanted to keep him.

Dominick gave me a glimpse of what it was like to be more than alone, and suddenly I wanted it all.

Throwing back the covers, I headed for the shower. It was time to get these thoughts, these feelings back under control.

We'd both agreed to a no-strings affair, and I wasn't going to be the one to change that. Rejection wasn't something I enjoyed, and what we had was better than nothing.

I lingered in the shower, gathering myself and trying to clear my head and turn off my heart. I emerged clean, sparkly, and determined.

Dominick was already in the kitchen and had made coffee.

"Good morning," he said, and pressed a light kiss to my forehead.

His lips traveled down my cheek and a slow, sweet, lingering kiss that had my heart jumping up and down was next.

"Morning." I reached for the coffee pot with shaking hands.

I perched my butt on the edge of a kitchen chair and eyed him over the full cup. "So, aside from last night, how you been lately?"

Cursing my happy heart, I reminded myself that he hadn't called or made any effort to see me for almost ten days before I'd finally called him with the invite to the dinner. This was a casual thing, not a love thing. I could *not* forget that.

"Amazingly well," he said. He moved across the floor and sat on the chair across from me. "And I have to thank you for that."

"What? Why?" Because I'd left him alone?

"Because you inspired me. And you challenged me." His lips lifted at one corner and my breath caught. His amber eyes were almost glowing with pride and pleasure.

"I inspired you? To do what? You're hair's the same, and I didn't notice any piercings when I licked you all over this morning."

He laughed and shook his head. "To go for it. To chase my dream. I've been writing, and not just that fluff article. I started a novel."

"Dominick! That's wonderful!" I jumped from my seat and hugged him. His hands circled my waist and pulled me across his lap.

"Thank you," he whispered against my lips.

"For what?" I stared into his eyes, drowning in the rightness of how it all felt.

"For being you. For chasing your dream, and for not being afraid to be true to your own artistic side. I love that you aren't afraid to be yourself."

My heart kicked and my stomach clenched. He loved that I was myself. He hadn't said he loved *me* . . . but it was close.

"I have a question for you, though."

"Shoot."

"Why do you only have one nipple pierced? Don't most people get both done?"

Heat crept up my neck. He thought I was so daring I didn't wanted to tell him the truth and ruin the image.

Oh, well. I wanted him to know all of me, so no secrets.

"I wasn't sure I'd like it. I mean—I loved the way it looked. My best friend Caitlyn has both of hers pierced, and she always complained about the lack of really nice, yet affordable decorations. She had to shop on the Net because there weren't any in the stores around here. So I made a couple of pieces for her, and she convinced me to get it done myself. Only, I wasn't sure I'd enjoy the sensations. My nipples are sensitive enough, so I only got one. As a tester."

"But you do like it."

It wasn't a question; we both knew that I loved it. When he toyed with my nipples, rings or not, it got me going every time. But I answered anyway. "I do. But I also like having only one. It's . . . different."

He laughed. "That's my girl!"

167

Pleasure swept over me at his words, and we met in another rousing kiss before he set me aside and stood up. "I have to go. What are you up to this afternoon? Do you have plans?"

I shook my head, burying my disappointment.

He grinned. "Will you meet me later? I have a surprise for you."

18

Dominick

"Dom, it's been almost a month and you still don't have another job. Get off your ass and do something already, would you?"

I grinned at the gorgeous brunette across the table from me. Teal was one of only two women—hell, the only two *people* I ever let talk to me that way.

Okay, that would be three now. If Mia wanted to curse at me, I'd probably let her. Shit, I'd let her do pretty much anything.

Then there was my father. I'd let my dad talk to me that way, too, but he never would. For some reason, only the women in the Jamison family loved to boss everyone around and try to control things. Us men just sat back and let them. It made life a lot easier.

Usually.

"Teal, you're my sister and I love you, but back off."

I picked up another piece of tuna maki and shoved it in my mouth. *Too bad I couldn't shove it in hers; it might keep her quiet.*

"No, I won't back off. I get why you quit *The City*. I even get why you turned down the other three papers, but you have to make a decision soon." She sighed and I felt what little resistance I had left soften at the concern in her light brown eyes. "You might be loving this mini vacation right now, but I know you, brother dear. It won't last."

Dare I tell her it's a woman and not the lack of job that had me so . . . wired?

Shit, no. If I told her I met a woman that I couldn't get off my mind, she'd never let it go. She'd probably track Mia down herself and demand to know why she wasn't in love with me.

No, it was best to keep the conversation focused on work. Maybe I could even sneak in my favor and she wouldn't think anything of it. "So how's the gallery?"

She glared at me, but there was pride in her posture, and I knew she wouldn't be able to hold back. "It's going great! After being open only three months, the costs of opening are almost cleared!"

"Good for you, sis. I knew you'd make it a success." Teal was nothing if not driven. She'd love that Mia was driven, too. They'd get along like long-lost sisters.

I gave my head a shake. Sisters? Talk about jumping the gun.

I sat back and contemplated the best way to approach this. Lush was Teal's baby. It was everything to her. If it weren't for the carpenter she'd fallen for when getting it set up, it would be the sole focus of her life.

Obviously, the relationship was doing her good, because she glowed with a vitality I hadn't seen in her since we were kids.

"It's not me," she said, still talking about the gallery. "I'm just providing space for all the wonderful artists out there. There's so many of them that have been looking for a place to feature their edgier pieces that I'm getting overloaded with stock."

"You're overstocked?"

"No, but I would be if it wasn't selling as fast as it came in."

Perfect.

"You really hit the market right, eh? And Zach? He still treating you like a queen?"

Color flooded her cheeks and she held up her left hand.

"Jesus, Teal! How did I miss that rock?" It had to be worth a fortune. Yellow gold band, big diamond, left hand. A grin spread across his face and happiness for her warmed him.

"You're a man. Men never notice these things."

"I'm happy for you." It had been obvious from the day I met him that Zach worshipped my sister. And when I'd made it clear that nothing less than worship would be good enough to keep Zach safe, the guy just grinned and said, "No problem."

He was a good guy.

"So, when are you going to tell me about her?"

I froze with a piece of sashimi halfway to my mouth. "About whom?"

"C'mon, Dom. You can't lie to me. There's more going on with you than being unemployed, and since you haven't brought whatever it is up, it must be a woman."

Her logic eluded me, but the witch was right.

Maybe I could tell her I was working on a novel, and while still technically unemployed, I was working. But, really, I wasn't ready to share that yet. It was special.

Mia was special, too, but suddenly, in light of my sister's new engaged status, it felt okay to talk about her. Besides, I wouldn't be able to keep her a secret forever, especially if everything went the way I wanted it to.

So I told her about Mia. Not all the details, of course. Just that I'd met a super sexy woman and we were seeing each other.

Teal laughed. "Met your match, have you?"

I scowled, then gave up and grinned like an idiot. "Yeah, I have. You're gonna love her."

Her eyebrows rose. "I get to meet her?"

Warmth crept up my neck. "Uhmm, yeah. Actually, you're going to meet her in about fifteen minutes. I asked her to drop by Lush."

Teal stared at me, her mouth opening and closing silently. Then she just said simply, "Let's get over there then."

Relief flooded me, and in that instant I truly understood how different my family was from Mia's. Teal would have her questions, but they weren't important. Not yet. The truth was, when it came down to it, they supported each other.

I stood and dropped some cash on the table for the sushi. "I'm not going to go in with you when we get back," I told her as we started the walk back to the gallery.

Teal frowned. "Why not?"

"I asked Mia to bring some samples of her work with her, but she doesn't know exactly why."

"Her work?"

I explained to Teal that Mia was a jewelry designer, and that most of her stuff was of the kinky or erotic variety. "She's just starting out, but she's got such passion for it."

"Dom, this is my business." Teal shook her head gently.

"I know," I interrupted. "I'm not asking you to sell it for her. I'm just asking you to look at it. I think she's got some great stuff, and it would be perfect for Lush. But I only want you to take her on as a client if you really believe in it."

"And I think you will," I tacked on after a short silence.

We reached the parking lot of Lush, and Teal stopped to give me a searching look.

"What?"

"You must really care about her to ask me to even look at it.

172

I know how you hate it when people try to use connections to get ahead."

I met her gaze head-on. "I do."

"I'll look at her stuff." She leaned in and gave me a big hug. "Thank you."

Suddenly anxious about how Mia would react, I stepped back and watched as Teal pulled open the door to the gallery. "You must be Mia! Sorry I'm late."

19

Mia

Pure adrenaline-laced joy kept me inches off the ground as I exited the erotic art gallery, Lush. Teal, the owner, and apparently Dominick's *sister* had greeted me warmly and explained why Dominick wasn't there and what was going on.

At first I hadn't been sure what to think. I'd been wandering around the gallery, fantasizing about several of the pieces there and hatching plans to book a sales meeting with the owner, only to find out I already had one.

As a favor to Dominick.

"I agreed to look at your samples and talk to you, but you need to know that no one tells me what to sell in my store. Including my brother," Teal had said. And I believed her.

I knew Dominick hated it when people used favors to get ahead or take shortcuts, and I could tell by her clear gaze and openness that Teal was determined to be fair. Friend of her brother or no.

"Perfect," I'd replied. "I'll take the meeting, I'm not an idiot. But I do want to sell on my own. I don't want favors."

With a clear understanding of where we each stood, I'd showed her what I had.

"Well? Are you going to tell me how it went or what?"

I snapped back to reality and saw Dominick leaning against his Mustang. Without a second thought I flew across the five feet separating us and launched myself into his arms. "She's going to sell me, well, my stuff. She also said she'd refer people to me for custom work. She has tons of ideas about marketing and everything. She loved me!"

A grin spread across his gorgeous face and he cupped my head in his hands. "I love you."

My heart stopped, then kicked so hard I thought it would come straight through my ribs. "You do?"

He laughed. "Yes, I do. This 'just sex' thing isn't going to work for me anymore. Do you think we can work something else out?"

"Something like what?"

He sobered. "Well, I guess that depends on how you feel about me."

I stared into his amber eyes, dark with uncertainty. How could he ever doubt how I felt? "I love you, too. I didn't plan to. I didn't even want to. Being alone is safer, but you . . . You make me feel safe, and loved, and whole. Last week, without you around and under my feet all the time, I was lonely."

He pulled me tight to him and I could feel our heartbeats meet and match in rhythm.

"I plan on being under your feet for a long time to come, darlin'."

Sexual Healing

1

Hard muscles, supple skin, and slow, firm strokes. Caitlyn Ellis knew that was what made a massage good. Not just for the receiver, but also for her, the giver.

The tensile strength rippling beneath oiled skin, responding to her slightest touch. The pleasurable sighs that filled the dimly lit room when she worked him over. Her thumbs digging in slightly, circling wider each time, followed by a more complete stroke with the heel of her hands. And finally, a smooth, healing caress of the hands skimming over everything.

The flow of energy from her hands easing the stress and pain of another made her body hum and her soul soar.

Energy came in many forms, from many sources. For Caitlyn, it was mostly sexual. She enjoyed her job as a massage therapist. She liked to heal people and bring them peace, and she drew on her own most basic energy source to do it.

Sexual energy.

Not all clients were as open and receptive to her energy as Ben was, but even if they were completely blocked to energy work, the technical aspect of a proper massage worked wonders.

The thing with Ben was, he was completely open to her, and each time she saw him, it became more and more potent. The sheet over his hips was always tented impressively at the end of a session; he made no attempts to hide it, and she was always damp and aching.

It would be natural for them to hook up. Ben had asked her out often, and idiot that she was, she'd always said no. He even said he'd go to another massage therapist if she'd only go out with him, but she stayed firm. She wasn't exactly sure why; after all, it wasn't like she was a fan of rules or restrictions.

She was, however, a woman who trusted her instincts. And the dull blue base of his overall aura told her he was a bit too content with his life, maybe even selfish. He certainly had no real ambition or drive for success, and that bothered her.

Plus, she was done with short-term flings.

"So, is the answer still the same, Cait?" Ben's voice was husky as he lay back on the table.

Caitlyn finished washing her hands in the sink and turned back to him with a small smile. "Sorry, Ben. The answer's always going to be no."

"I know you like me." He tucked one hand beneath his head as he spoke, his other hand inching toward the edge of his sheet.

Her pulse picked up a bit of speed. She'd often wondered if he masturbated after she left. She usually did, because her body would be humming on a high note if she didn't. The thought of him doing it at the same time had been a regular fantasy when she'd played with herself.

"I do like you," she said finally. And she did, mostly. Especially his body. "But I'm not going to change my mind. You and I would not be a good match."

A hot body was nice, but it wasn't everything. She might feel a sexual pull low in her belly when she was giving him a massage, but other than that, there was no spark. If she hadn't given up on one-night stands a long time ago, she might've considered him for one, but that was in the past. She'd grown a lot, and she wasn't willing to just give herself away anymore.

"You know you want me." His eyelids lowered and his voice dropped, then so did his sheet.

It seemed Ben was tired of being a good boy and taking no for an answer. Caitlyn leaned back against the sink and prepared to enjoy the show. She knew she shouldn't, but well, sometimes people did things they knew they shouldn't. It was a fact of life.

His cock was long, strong, and standing proud. He circled his shaft with his thumb and forefinger and stroked up and down the length slowly. She could see the head darkening in color, and arousal hummed through her veins, settling between her thighs.

Caitlyn was no innocent; she'd had her wild days and nights, and just because she was looking for more than a sexual fling didn't mean she couldn't enjoy a free show. As long as he understood that's all it would be.

"Very nice," she said. "I've always had a bit of a voyeuristic streak."

Ben smiled and his lovely blue eyes twinkled mischievously. He bent his knee, angling his leg out to the side so she could see everything, and her sex pulsed. Caitlyn knew he was watching her as she monitored his movements and she was watching him.

Caitlyn's fingers curled into the palms of her hands. It had been too long since she'd held the heated throb of an aroused man in her hand. Saliva pooled in her mouth, and heat crept over her chest and up her neck.

"You really do like to watch, don't you?" he murmured.

She nodded, licking her lips as his fist tightened and the head of his cock darkened. He pumped his hand up and down, his speed picking up enough that she knew he was close. On every upstroke, he curled his hand over the crown and her tongue was starting to twitch; she really wanted to be the one playing with him.

Or even playing with herself.

She pressed her thighs together and flexed her inner muscles, but there was no relief. She'd have to wait until she was alone. Not because she was shy, but because she was at work, and her professionalism meant a lot to her. Well, enough to inch only a toe across the line, and not her whole foot.

"I can feel your eyes on me. It's almost like it's you stroking me. So good, Cait. We could be so good together. Just once, come on over here and help me."

She shook her head. Tense. Waiting. His aura was vibrating, shifting with his energy; there was a flush across his cheek-bones, and his panting was noticeable. His hand twisted just a little on each upstroke, and she could see the vein on the underside throbbing.

"Come for me," she whispered.

And he did.

She watched as he threw his head back on the table, his hips arched up, and his fist tightened. Semen jumped from his cock and Cait's insides trembled.

"Yes!" he hissed.

He released his cock and his hand fell to his side. Caitlyn turned back to the sink and put a facecloth under the warm water. When it was soaked, she turned off the taps, squeezed out the cloth, and stepped over to him. She placed the cloth on his belly and bent down to place a soft kiss on his lips.

"Thank you."

She turned and left the room, knowing she wouldn't accept another appointment with him. He was good-looking, nice enough, but she knew he only wanted her as long as he couldn't have her . . . and she wanted more than that from a man.

2

She was late.

Damn it. She hated being late. To Caitlyn, lateness was just plain rude. People who said they were always late "no matter what" were people who didn't care about others, even as a common courtesy.

In this case, she was late for two reasons. Okay, really it was one reason. She wasn't sure being the model for her best friend's line of erotic body decorations was a good idea. And because she was unsure, she'd let herself get distracted by Ben, therefore making herself late. And testy.

Her energy was super high, and she was strung tight. Part of it was frustration from watching Ben and not being able to take care of herself. If she'd been smart enough to carry the silly little pocket rocket she had, maybe she'd have been able to give herself a little quick TLC.

But part of her also felt like something big was about to happen. There was a small burn of anticipation running through her.

She gave herself a mental shake. Oh well, life goes on. Really, she could masturbate anytime, but these photos meant a lot to Mia, and she'd already had to postpone once, she wouldn't do it again.

Cait finished climbing the stairs to Jack Lowell's studio loft and knocked on the door.

Big place. She wondered if there were other studios like it available in the building. One with a window facing east for the sunshine would be wonderful. She could maybe finally have her own little holistic healing center; she'd only need a tiny space for a bedroom, and the rest of the loft would be work-space.

As she was peeking around to see if there were any other doors or apartments, the one behind her opened.

"It's about time you got here." The voice was deep and harsh, as if it were rusty from disuse.

Caitlyn turned back to the studio loft and stared at the man there. He had short, dark blond hair that was mussed and spiked up all over, not in a style, but in a who-gives-a-damn way. He had on jeans and a gray T-shirt and looked somewhat presentable, except for the black wisps drifting through his aura.

The man was messed up. The light base told her he was intelligent. He was physically fit, but the location and movement of the darkness told her he was feeling pretty negative, even depressed.

"Jack Lowell?"

"Who else would be answering my door? Come in already. You're late."

Charming, too, she thought as she walked into the loft. When she was close enough to see past the photographer's facial hair and scowl, she almost gasped at the beautiful green eyes. Surrounded by long, thick eyelashes, his piercing gaze gave the impression he could see everything. And the shadows she saw flickering in them told her he had seen a lot.

Enough to cast the darkness she saw in his soul.

Jack shut the door behind the woman and wondered what the hell Teal had been thinking to send him an overweight model.

Then he heaved a mental sigh and decided it was none of his business. Teal Jamison might be a friend who was kind enough to send him some commercial work to help pay his bills, but she was also her own businesswoman, and a smart one. So he'd just take the pictures and mind his own business.

Besides, this was a one-time only thing for him. He photographed objects, not people. What did he know about models?

"There's a screen over there," he said, and pointed to the corner of the room next to his drop cloth setup. "You can get undressed there."

She stood in the middle of the room, gazing around for a minute before she turned to him and held out her hand. "I'm Caitlyn Ellis."

"I know."

Her eyes ran over him and he was suddenly aware that he hadn't shaved for days. A shiver ran down his spine and he wondered what she saw. He'd showered; he was clean.

She had a strange expression on her face, and he wondered if she was nervous about posing for him. "You're safe to get undressed, but if you want to call a friend so you're not alone with me, I'll wait." *I'll be pissed off, but I'll wait.*

"No," she shook her head. "I'm fine with you. Where do I undress?"

He pointed to the corner again and she turned and went toward it. When she was behind the screen, he listened to the sounds of her clothes coming off and fought the urge to sneak a shot of whiskey. He had a bottle of Jack Daniels in the kitchen area and the craving was strong.

"Do you take a lot of nude portraits?" she asked as she came out from behind the screen.

Holy shit!

She hadn't bothered with a robe, and she walked over the center of the drop cloth completely naked and natural. Big, beautiful breasts were the first things he noticed. Then, the fact that they were both pierced with sapphire-tipped studs. Shanks? Barbells. That's what they were called, a barbell.

"You didn't bring a robe?" He tried not to stare. He'd seen naked women before. Plenty of them, in fact.

But Caitlyn was beautiful. She reminded him of those old oil paintings of well-rounded Renaissance women stretched out decadently on a chaise lounge. Lush and sensual, with soft, creamy skin that was made for a man's touch. And a completely shaven pussy.

He swallowed and tried not to notice his body's reaction.

"No. Was I supposed to?"

"It's my understanding most models do. So they have something to wear while we stand around and wait." He tore his gaze away from her and strode to the table where his camera was. "Then again, I don't normally work with models, so what do I know?"

"Wait? What are we waiting for?"

"We need the marks from your bra and panties to fade. They'll show up double in the photos." At least he remembered that from his schooling a lifetime ago.

He didn't bother to turn around. He could feel her presence in the studio and knew she hadn't left the drop cloth area.

"Oh."

Thankfully, she was silent while he pretended to focus on his equipment. Doing commercial shoots strained his patience, but not his knowledge.

In his opinion, the best photos were real. They didn't need filters or special lenses to make them look good, but he still had the gadgets to play with, if that's what the client wanted.

He snapped the wide-angle lens on his camera and called out over his shoulder. "You ready?"

"Just tell me what to do. I've never modeled before."

Great. Just great.

The longing for a shot of J.D. hit him again and he pushed it aside. He walked over to the woman and eyed her skin, ignoring the way it made his hands itch to touch. His cock twitched, but he ignored it, too. Time to work.

"The panty lines are gone, so we can start with some close-ups of the waist thing. After we get those, we can move on to the nipple rings and do the full body shots last. Are you okay with that?"

He supposed he should start slow since she'd never modeled before. But if she didn't mind strutting around naked in front of him, she shouldn't flinch at starting with the close-ups.

"Okay. Do you just want me to stand straight or what?"

He directed her into the light and had her pose, lifting her arms out of the shot so he could get the curve of her waist, the silver link chain dipping over her soft belly.

"Next one," he said, trying not to breathe too deeply. She was aroused. He could smell it when he was close to her, and the scent was going straight to his dick.

He could feel her looking at him as she changed chains, but he avoided her gaze. Her nipples were hard and changing color, darkening with her arousal and looking in need of attention. What would it feel like to run his tongue over those nipples and tug on the piercing with his teeth?

When she had it on, he took the same shots. "Turn," he said curtly, after taking a couple of shots from the front and sides.

She turned, slowly and he focused on the curve of her back and the intricate clasp of the thing. What was it with women that made them think sparkly things were needed to make them look good?

He stepped back. "You have another one?"

"One more waist chain. Mia asked me to bring three of each thing to show some various styles. She said her and Teal would pick what ones to use in their marketing campaign later."

She turned, and the tinkle of her ankle bracelet rang in his ears. Around her waist, the newest chain, a single strand so silver it was almost white, was decorated with several smaller ones draping off it so that they fell softly across her lower belly and over her hips. It was simple and flowing. It made him think of . . . Shit, that's a great photo idea!

"Hang on," he said. He took a couple of quick shots of the chain, then set his camera aside. He went through the whole loft and grabbed every pillow he could find, including the crappy beanbag chair from the TV room. He tossed them all against the backdrop, using the pillows to cover the beanbag chair.

"Lay down," he told her, picking up his camera again.

She looked at the pillows, looked at him, then looked at the chain. When her lips split into a sultry smile, he knew she'd figured out what he had in mind.

3

Caitlyn lowered herself to the ground and lounged back against the mound of pillows Jack had built. All she needed was a silk scarf to use as a veil and the fantasy scene would be complete. She'd never really caught the harem look of the chain and its draping style until Jack's eyes had lit up and he'd started piling up the pillows.

Wanting to get into the mood, into the fantasy, she closed her eyes. She imagined the warmth of the sun filtering through tent walls and the quiet of a desert hideaway. She imagined she was nothing more than a concubine laid out to await her master's pleasure.

Cailtyn's earlier arousal came back threefold. It swamped her, warming her body. Making it pliant and supple. She opened her eyes and looked at the man in front of her. Tall, rugged . . . almost dangerous. His build told her his body was strong, and his posture said he knew how to use it.

She lowered her eyelids seductively as he came closer. She couldn't see his eyes, but she didn't need to. She could hear his breathing, see his aura shift, and feel the energy vibrate in the air between them. He wasn't completely open, but he wasn't completely closed off to her energy either.

He could feel what she was putting out there, she could tell, and it stoked her inner fires even more.

A twist of her hips and she shifted position.

Lifting a hand, she trailed her fingertips lightly over her breast and watched him focus his attention there. She played with one nipple for a moment, then the other. Abandoning the hard buds, she slowly trailed her hands up and down over her ribs and chest. The light touch, the whisper of a nail scraping across her skin, heightened her sensitivity.

She pressed one palm flat and slid it over her belly, past the chain that marked her as his property, and over the smooth, hairless skin of her pubes.

The temperature in the tent heated, and the silence was broken only by their breathing. Closing her eyes and opening her legs, she ran a finger up and down her slit. She dipped it in a little and spread her juices around, teasing herself . . . and him.

Soon her clit was begging for attention and she couldn't ignore it anymore.

With slow, deliberate movements, she began to rub it, side to side, then in a gentle circle. Her other hand cupped a full breast, squeezed it, and tweaked the rigid peak with her thumb. Bolts of pleasure shot to her core and she sighed.

She felt him, felt his presence close to her, watching, enjoying, no, reveling in the sight she made, the energy she was releasing. And she reveled in the knowledge that she was pleasing him.

Flattening her palm, she slid a finger the length of her folds and into her body. Her sex clenched and she added another finger. Her hips began to rotate and lift. The heel of her hand pressed against her clit and sensations swept over her. Everything started to tighten—her muscles, her focus, her pleasure.

She threw her head back, arched her back, and tugged on the nipple ring. A flash of pain-laced pleasure whipped through her and her insides convulsed. Sparks went off behind her eyes, and she cried out as her sex clamped down on her fingers, extending her orgasm.

Satisfaction made her body limp. She closed her legs on her hand and curled onto her side. When her heart stopped pounding and the fireworks behind her eyes faded, she opened her eyes to see, not her fantasy sheik stripping off his clothes in preparation of taking her, but Jack the photographer with a soul that needed healing.

A spirit that was reaching out.

She'd known for some time that there had to be someone special out there for her. Someone who would not only be open to her, but who would need her, and most of all . . . want her.

When she looked at Jack Lowell, she knew it was him. His aura was reaching out to her. She could see that it had already absorbed some of her energy, and was hungry for more. And instead of feeling drained, as she always did when she put out so much energy that another could hold on to it, she felt energized.

She was drawn to Jack in a way she'd never been drawn to another. It was more than sexual, more than spiritual. It was mystical . . . almost magical.

She felt more balanced than she'd ever been in her whole life.

Only he still had those dark threads weaving around him. He was open psychically to her energy, but he probably wasn't even aware of it. He was mentally closed off and spiritually damaged. If she wanted any sort of future with him, she needed a way in. And her strongest way was through his most basic need.

The need that was glowing in his eyes right then.

The need for sexual satisfaction.

193

4

———

Jack was lost.

What was he supposed to do? His dick was harder than a fence post, and his brain was numb.

"Did you get some good photos?" Her voice was husky and her lips were tilted up just a bit.

Was she laughing at him?

Did he care if she was?

The answer to that shocked him. He did care. He didn't want her to be laughing at him.

"I think I have everything I need," he said. *Except a fucking drink.*

He walked back to his worktable and set down the camera.

When she'd first started to touch herself, he'd kept snapping shots; but when she'd really gotten into it, her hips moving and her body flushing with arousal, he'd forgotten about the camera and just watched.

She'd been absolutely amazing. He'd never seen something—someone—so beautiful. So sensual and erotic.

He'd seen women masturbate before. But Caitlyn had fairly

glowed with her arousal. It didn't matter that he'd always been attracted to slim, strong women, and she was a good bit overweight. It didn't matter that her breasts were big and her hips were bigger.

What had mattered was her innate sexuality. Her confidence, the translucence of her skin, the flush of desire that had colored her chest and neck; he'd watched it creep up and over her cheeks. When he'd watched her bite down on her lip, he'd wanted to be the one doing it.

There was no more doubt in his mind about why Teal had wanted her to be the nude model.

A hand came down lightly on his shoulder and his body jerked tight. "Are you all right?"

He closed his eyes. "Of course, I'm all right. I've just got a hard-on I could hammer nails with thanks to you."

"I couldn't help myself. Didn't you enjoy watching me?"

Jack bit his lip. What was he supposed to say to that? For whatever reason, he was trying not to be a complete asshole to her.

"I enjoyed you watching me," she said softly.

"Yeah, I noticed."

"Why won't you look at me?"

Why was she still talking to him? Why hadn't she walked away?

"I'm working. You know, doing the job I was hired to do?" As if to prove his point, he snapped on the lens guard and set the camera in its case.

She didn't say anything else, and she didn't leave. As far as he could tell, she didn't even move. She just stood behind him, close enough for the heat of her body to warm his back.

Finally, unable to stand it anymore, he turned and faced her. "What?"

Her blue, blue eyes were soft, and she spoke gently. "I want to make you feel better."

"You're crazy," he choked out.

"No, I'm not." She stepped closer, placed her hand on his cheek, and looked up at him with caring eyes. "I feel a connection with you that I refuse to walk away from. It's the kind of connection I've been waiting for."

"A connection, huh?" He snorted. What the fuck did *that* mean? "What you're feeling is horny, babe."

She traced her fingers across his lips and he could smell her juices there. His blood heated and he gave a sharp nod. A man could only take so much. If she was willing, he wasn't going to say no.

"You want to make me feel better?" With one quick move he grabbed her by the waist, spun, and pinned her to the table. "Spread your legs."

He expected her to slap him at the very least. Instead, she slid her hand behind his head and pulled him to her.

With a groan, he gave in, slanting his mouth over hers. His tongue thrust between her soft lips, and he took what he wanted. There was no slow and gentle, he wanted hot and deep in every way.

She rubbed against him, meeting him, moving with him, letting him take control. Warmth started to seep through his skin, spreading from her to him. Wherever she touched, heat followed. She ran her fingers through his hair and pressed her chest to his, the hard rocks of her nipples calling to him. He tore his mouth from hers, cupped those big beauties, and lifted them for his mouth.

He squeezed the soft flesh and ran his tongue over the nipples, toying with the jewelry. He went from one to the other while she tugged his shirt from his jeans and lifted it. He backed away and let her pull it over his head, then boosted her onto the counter, unzipped his pants, and stepped between her legs.

Her eyes were watching him, desire and something else, something softer, making him think she could see right through him. Like she could see into his heart and knew that it was just a shell.

Who cares? he thought. She wasn't interested in his heart, just a fuck.

He dipped a hand between her thighs, felt the slick heat there, and saw her shiver. She was ready for him.

"The only connection we have is that you're hot and wet, and I'm hard and horny." He thrust his hips and entered her easily. Her hands gripped his shoulders, her legs wrapped around his waist, and she stared at him while he thrust in and pulled out.

After two strokes, his control was gone. She felt so damned good. So hot, and wet, and tight. Safe. She felt safe and wonderful. He closed his eyes and threw his head back, unable to look at her. He pumped his hips, faster and faster, feeling her tightness give and welcome him home each time.

"Fuck," he grunted. "I'm not going to last long, woman."

Her hands curled and her fingers dug into his skin. "Come for me, Jack. It's okay."

He pumped faster, pulling her closer, holding her tight to him as his strokes shortened. He was barely leaving her body now. He didn't ever want to leave.

"Come, Jack," she whispered again. And he did.

His mind went blank, his control snapped, and everything in him rushed to his cock. He swelled, felt her insides clutch at him, massage him and take everything he had to give.

Then he was empty.

Suddenly, his body was heavy and his muscles weak. He fell forward, resting his head on the curve of her shoulder as her arms wrapped around him. She held him, skin to skin, heart to heart, and his pulse slowed. He could've slept like that, standing up and cradled against her soft body.

5

"These are fantastic, Jack. I knew you were the right one for this project."

Jack took another pull from his beer and eyed the pretty brunette across the table as she flipped through some of the proofs from his photo shoot with Caitlyn. He hadn't brought *all* of them. Some were only for his eyes.

"It went better than I expected." Even Caitlyn's exit had gone better than he'd expected. When he'd pulled away from her and zipped his pants, he'd expected her to want to talk. Women always wanted to talk, and talking was the last thing he'd wanted to do. But Caitlyn had just gotten dressed and left. She'd even given him a small kiss on the cheek on her way out the door. The woman was not normal. "How well do you know the model you sent? Caitlyn Ellis."

Teal raised her head and pinned him with a stare. "I've only met her a couple of times; she's a friend of the jewelry designer. Did you two hit it off?"

He shrugged and took another drink from his beer. "She was . . . interesting."

"That's a good way to describe her," Teal said with a chuckle. She set aside the photos and met his gaze. She looked good, real good. She looked relaxed, her amber eyes mellow with a contentment he'd never seen on her before. "The first time I met her, she knew I had a headache within seconds. She just looked at me and knew it. She sat me down in a corner of the back room, did something with her hands for a couple minutes, and my headache disappeared. And that was a bad headache, too, the start of a doozy of a migraine."

Jack didn't say anything to that. What could he say? He wasn't a particular believer in the supernatural or extrasensory. But he'd also seen things that couldn't be explained.

As if sensing his thoughts, Teal leaned forward and spoke softly, "Dare I hope she pricked your interest?"

"Is that why you wanted me to do the photo shoot when you know I'm not the artistic type?" He swallowed a sigh and gave her a blank stare. "Fifteen years as a photojournalist doesn't make me a good art photographer, Teal. In fact, it doesn't make me good for much else."

"You have the eye, Jack. You just need to want to do it. Besides, tell me I was wrong and there was no chemistry between you and Caitlyn."

"So which ones you want printed?" He gestured to the proofs and moved the conversation along.

With a shake of her head, Teal selected the ones she wanted for her ads. After trying to get him to talk about Caitlyn one more time, she stood and gave him a hug. "You're hopeless, Jack."

Teal had always been a beauty, and a smart one, too. She left the pub, and he ordered another beer. Jack knew she was right about one thing: He *was* hopeless.

He'd always had a good eye for photography. It was what

always put his photos on the covers of magazines like *Time* or *Newsweek*. But years of taking pictures of kids toting around automatic weapons and soldiers cradling dead babies with decimated cities in the background made it hard to see the pretty things most people wanted photos of, and easy to give up hope.

"Cait! I have no idea why, but you've shocked me."

Caitlyn watched as Mia poured another glass of wine for each of them. She hadn't really shocked her friend; they knew each other too well for that. Besides, it was pretty hard to shock a redheaded wild child like Mia.

"You must be getting stodgy in your couplehood if that shocks you. Used to be you'd be the one telling me to loosen up."

"I'm not stodgy!"

"Really? When was the last time you did anything crazy and unexpected? Anything truly Mia-like?"

"Remember that weekend getaway Dom took me on a couple of weeks ago? Well, it was just to Calgary, but the bar across from the hotel was having an amateur strip contest . . ."

"You entered it?" Caitlyn smiled. Mia looked the wild child, she even acted it a lot, but deep down, she'd always wanted just one thing: a home and a family to belong to. She'd found that with Dominick, and Caitlyn was glad Dom enjoyed her friend's adventurous side, too.

"No, but I watched it with Dom, then took him into a back room for a private lap dance." Mia's grin was full of pride.

"I do love the way you dance," Dominick Jamison said as he strolled into the kitchen. "When the house is built, I'm getting Zach to install a pole for you."

Dominick was Mia's significant other. They'd only met two months ago, but anyone who saw them together knew that this was it. They were forever. Caitlyn could clearly see the love that surrounded them, and their auras were blending. They were a perfect match, balancing each other out.

"What are you two talking about that requires you telling her that story anyway?" He reached into the cupboard and pulled out a tin. He glanced over his shoulder at the girls and started to make coffee.

Dom's thick dark hair was mussed and his jaw unshaven. He was working in the other room, in the middle of editing his first novel before having his new agent send it out. Which kept him out of the way while Caitlyn and Mia had their girls' chat over some wine and snacks.

Mia raised an eyebrow in Cailtyn's direction. Caitlyn nibbled at a cracker and shrugged.

"Caitlyn did the photo shoot for my designs yesterday with Teal's friend Jack, and while she was *posing*, she got a little carried away."

Dominick leaned against the kitchen counter and waited for the coffee to finish brewing. "Jack Lowell? That's who she got to do your pictures?"

Cait's pulse jumped. "Yes, do you know him?"

"Yeah, he and Teal were an item for a while, long time ago. I knew they kept in touch, but I didn't know Jack was back in town. And he took your pictures?" He shook his head, surprised.

"Why are you surprised? Teal said he was a great photographer," Mia asked.

"He is. But he's a photojournalist, not a fashion photographer."

"And you used to be a columnist, not a fiction novelist. Don't pigeonhole him."

Dominick grinned at Mia. "I'm not, baby. I'm sure if Teal sent her to Jack, she knew what she was doing."

"What else do you know about him?" Caitlyn tried to keep her voice casual.

"I'll tell you what I know if you tell me what Mia meant by 'carried away.' " He waggled his eyebrows.

Mia laughed and shook a finger at Dom, but Cait wasn't worried. She let a small smile lift her lips and she told him she'd masturbated for Jack during the shoot.

"He asked you to do that?"

"No, I just had the urge and followed it."

Dominick looked from Caitlyn to Mia and back. Then he left the room shaking his head and chuckling softly.

Caitlyn wanted to yell at him that he hadn't told her anything about Jack yet, but Mia beat her to it.

"Oh, sorry." Dom stuck his head around the corner again. "Not much to tell. When he and Teal were together, he was always away on some assignment, so it never lasted. Then again, that might be why they remained friends. My sister was never into long term until she met Zach. Anyway, I met him a couple times, good guy, great sense of humor."

A great sense of humor?

Dom still stood in the doorway with coffee mug in hand, amber eyes questioning. Caitlyn smiled and waved him away. She was dying to know more about Jack, but she'd find it out herself.

6

Caitlyn checked her appearance in the mirror one last time before grabbing her keys and heading out the door. Four days had passed since the photo shoot, and she hadn't seen or heard from Jack.

She hadn't really expected to, but that didn't stop the disappointment from settling in her stomach.

She'd made light of her actions with Mia and Dom, but really, Jack had touched her. At first it had just been the urge to soothe; his dark aura called to the healer in her. But things had somehow shifted until she wanted to do more than heal him.

She wanted to love him.

It was sudden and inexplicable, but there it was. She truly believed there was no such thing as a coincidence, and their meeting was the perfect example.

She'd always been aware of her sexuality. She was pretty, but with an extra thirty pounds on her frame, nothing special in the looks department. Yet, men were always attracted to her.

When she was in her teens, she started to see clouds of color around people. When she and Mia had gone to a psychic fair in hope of having their fortunes told, she'd found a guy who did "energy work." He'd recognized something in her and asked her if she saw the colors. When she'd answered yes, he spent the rest of the night ignoring patrons and talking to her about auras and telling her she was gifted.

As she grew older and she'd studied everything she could about auras, charkas, and energy balancing, she learned that she was strongest when she was turned on. Sex wasn't something she'd ever shied away from, but when she'd connected the dots in her own self, everything had become stronger.

At first she'd gone a little crazy with it. For a year, almost two, she'd been pretty casual with her sexual adventures until she realized that it was draining her, not feeding her. Sex was pleasurable enough, but she didn't need a partner for pleasure. What she wanted, what she really needed, was true intimacy.

And until she found that, she'd given up on casual sex. That had been almost a year ago.

Masturbating for Jack had been the most intimate thing she'd ever done. Even more so than watching Ben do it for her. Ben had done it for himself. He'd done it to get off. Caitlyn had done it because, somehow, she knew it was what Jack had been thinking as he'd snapped those photos of her lounging on the pillow.

The desert sheik fantasy had come out of nowhere for her . . . but she went with it. She'd wanted the pleasure of it for herself, and for the man watching her.

When he'd emptied himself into her, Caitlyn had felt her heart swell. She'd held Jack to her and he'd clutched her tight. She was sure it was an unconscious thing for him, but somehow, somewhere inside him, he hadn't wanted to let go. She'd sensed it in his hot breath on her neck and the heart pounding in his chest.

As she parked in front of the building that housed Jack's loft, her pulse raced and her palms dampened.

He wouldn't be eager to see her again. She knew this. But it wasn't going to stop her. She'd wanted to talk when she'd held him, to whisper and soothe him, but she knew he'd not welcome it. The walls around his heart were thick, high, and strong, and it was going to take more than a quickie to get to him. And he'd never be capable of loving someone—of loving her—until he learned to share his inner pain.

Which is why she was back in front of his building again.

She wanted him, and she was going to get him.

Someone was pounding on his head.

Shit, someone was knocking on the door. Jack pulled himself off the sofa and shuffled to the door. "I'm coming!" he shouted when the knocking continued. "Shut up already!"

He didn't have any appointments, but that didn't mean it wasn't a downstairs neighbor or something. He pretty much kept to himself, but some people still knew he was there. He pulled open the door and saw the woman who'd been on his mind almost constantly for the past few days.

His gut clenched and his mind went blank. Was he dreaming?

"Hi, Jack," she said when he remained silent. "Want to come out and play?"

When she'd left the loft he didn't think he'd ever see her again. The knowledge that he could if he wanted to, all he had to do was call Teal and ask for Caitlyn's number, had crouched in his head until he'd drank himself to sleep almost every night. Unfortunately, that still left him most of the daylight hours to think about her.

"Jack?" Her eyes dimmed, going from cheerfully bright to . . . determined. "Okay, if you won't come out, I'm coming in."

She marched past him and his nose twitched at her fresh scent. He shut the door and scrubbed a hand over his face. "Excuse me," he mumbled and headed for the bathroom.

He cranked the taps on and splashed cold water on his face. He brushed his teeth and sniffed at his shirt. He smelled okay; he looked okay. He needed to shave, but some women found that sexy.

His movements stalled and he looked at the man in the mirror. What the hell did he care? He hadn't been shaved last time he saw her, and she'd liked him just fine enough then.

Jack strode past the studio part of the loft and over to his living area. He found Caitlyn standing in front of his bookshelf checking up on his tastes. "Find what you're looking for?"

She turned to him with a smile. "You tell me. I'm looking for a date."

"Sorry, I don't do dates."

"You've already done me, so I think we can say that's not going to be a problem."

Despite himself, Jack felt his lips twitch. She was quick.

Surprising himself, he planted his hands on his hips and gave her the once-over. "What, exactly, did you have in mind?" She looked damn good in those tight jeans and a loose top that hung low on her neck. The cleavage was making his mouth water and his cock stir.

"There's a big, dumb action flick out that I'd like to see, but I don't want to go alone. Why don't you keep me company?"

A movie? He hadn't been to a movie in . . . well, in a long time. Fuck. He must be brain-dead. He didn't want anyone thinking they could be part of his life in any way, yet there he was, thinking with his dick again. Thinking it had felt damn good to be inside her the other day and wanting to bury himself in that warm, dark, loving place again.

"I'm not one for company, but if you ever want another fuck, you come see me again."

She didn't even flinch.

"I'll make you a deal." She looked him right in the eye as she moved closer. The heat was coming off her in waves and his body was responding to it, ready to deal with whatever terms she laid down. "You go to the movie with me, and I'm yours for the rest of the night."

Instant hard-on.

He narrowed his eyes, ignoring the way his heart was pumping and his pulse was pounding. "What makes you think that's a deal for me? You came to see me, not the other way around."

Her lips tipped in a small smile as she reached out and ran a finger over his distended zipper. "This makes me think it's a deal for you."

"Should I feel special, or are you always so forward?" He fought not to press himself more firmly into her hand and wondered what her game was. Nothing was ever as it seemed. He'd learned that the hard way. "Or should I say easy?"

She cocked her head to the side and a lock of hair brushed her cheek. "Easy? No. Forward? When I want something, yes."

"And is it often you see something you want? Should I be worried we didn't use a condom the other day?"

"It was almost a year for me, and I'm clean and safe. How about you?"

"I'm clean."

"And how long has it been since you've gotten what you wanted?" She leaned in, her lips brushing against his ear as she whispered, "How long has it been since you got what you needed?"

All the little hairs on his body stood on end, and he closed his eyes for a moment. With a quick shake of his head he stepped back and pinned her with a look. "I don't need anything. It was you who came to me, remember?"

"Yes, I came to you. Are you going to give me what I want?"

"A date or a fuck?"

"Both."

7

Caitlyn thought the movie was a brilliant idea. Get Jack out with her, but there wouldn't be any real pressure to talk. Even though she was dying to know more about him, part of her knew she had all the time in the world to learn what made him tick.

His defensive behavior at the loft hadn't put her off him at all. In fact, she was wondering if maybe she was a bit of a masochist because it just made her more determined.

Maybe, if he truly had the aura of an asshole or an evil person, but he didn't. It was dark and shadowed, but she'd seen it shift. He was attracted to her physically, for sure. But he was also piqued mentally.

His energy had kicked up a notch when she'd mentioned the movie, and it had tripled when she'd taken everything he'd dished out without missing a beat.

"I'll drive," he said when they reached the sidewalk.

"My truck's right here." She pointed at the shiny little Toyota.

"I'll still drive," he said, and held his hand out for the keys.

With a shrug, she handed him the keys and waited for him to open the door.

And like a gentleman, he did, waiting for her to climb in before closing it behind her and walking around to his side.

"Why a baby truck? Why not a real one?" he asked as he cranked it over.

"I love my little truck. I can haul my bed anywhere I go with no trouble, and it's still got great mileage."

He turned and stared at her. "Haul your *bed* anywhere you go?"

She could swear he was almost smiling. "My massage bed. Some call it a table. I'm a massage therapist."

"Part of this deal was anything I want later, right?"

She laughed. "Yes, it was. So, if you want a massage, I promise it will be one you never forget." Her palms actually itched to have him stretched out naked and oiled, ready for her touch.

He nodded and kept driving. The silence in the truck as he found the theater and parked was comfortable, and she knew they were on the right track. When they got their tickets, he paid; then he tried to put up a fight when she wanted to pay for the popcorn.

"I invited you out," she said, nudging him away from the counter with her hip. "Let me pay."

He stepped aside and smacked her lightly on the ass. "Stubborn wench."

She smiled at the teenage boy behind the counter and handed him her money. Jack might act like an asshole, but his manners and etiquette showed that he really was a gentleman.

8

Jack let Caitlyn pick where they'd sit. It had been so long since he'd been in a theater that he didn't even know where he liked to sit. He watched movies on TV, or rented DVDs occasionally, but he hadn't thought to visit a theater in a long while.

That didn't stop him from ragging on Caitlyn about her need to sit in the middle of the theater, though. Or the fact that she wanted chocolate M&M's while he liked peanut. He could not seem to stop picking at her, but she took it all in stride.

When they were seated, she handed him the popcorn to hold. "Take this," she'd commanded.

And he had. She settled into her seat and tucked the M&M's away in the cup on the far side.

"What? You're not going to share those?"

"You said you liked the peanut ones."

"Yeah, but I could eat those chocolate ones in a pinch." He didn't really want any. He was just enjoying their verbal sparring.

"You should've got your own. I told you to get your own."

"I thought you were going to share," he muttered.

She looked at him with slitted eyes and he stared back. When she held out the open package for him, he shook his head. "No, thanks."

She heaved a fake sigh and rolled her eyes. "Did I pass?"

"You're doing all right." He grinned at her as the lights dimmed and the trailers started to play.

The bickering had helped ease the tension between his shoulders and he relaxed back in his seat to watch the movie.

It started out okay, a couple making love, always a good way to start. An unrealistic but entertaining car chase. Each time their fingers brushed when they both reached into the popcorn bucket his body temperature went up a notch.

Then one of the heroes, a young kid, had to go and join the army. He wondered if kids were really given that as an option when they got caught breaking the law? If so, the judges should really warn them that they might survive the army better physically, but chances were they'd lose part of their soul in a war.

The last two years faded away as Jack watched the kid go through basic training, then ship off to war. His gut clenched and bile crept up his throat. He knew what was coming. He watched with the rest of the audience as the hero went from gung ho recruit to panic-stricken kid to disillusioned man covered in blood, sweat, and tears.

Tension crept back into every molecule of his body, and he fought the despair building inside him.

People in the audience thought the movie was sad, they felt pain and sympathy for the young soldier on the screen, but to them it was a good movie. The explosions weren't real; the bullets didn't really kill people, especially innocent people. It was entertainment.

They might even think bits and pieces of it were real . . . when, in reality, he knew that what they were seeing didn't even come close to the ugly truth of what was happening out in the world.

His chest was tight and his heart was pounding so hard he thought it would break his ribs. He sucked air in, and just as he was about to push out of is seat, a warm hand covered his on his thigh, and Caitlyn leaned her head against his shoulder.

She didn't say a word or look at him. She just touched him. Her thumb rubbed against the side of his thigh and warmth spread from there, blanketing him.

Air filled his lungs, and slowly his heart rate returned to normal. He was still tense. Too tense. Every muscle in his body hard as a rock. But his heart was calm, and his mind was getting there.

Caitlyn felt the change in Jack during the movie. It was a slow, progressive thing until she thought he was going to jump out of his skin. She'd put her hand on him, laid her head against his shoulder, and concentrated. She sent warm, healing energy through to him and felt the negative flow from him.

Not all of it, but enough that he was calm.

When they left the theater, she didn't try to make him talk, and he didn't offer any words. They drove in silence, and Caitlyn wondered if he would invite her in. Jack parked in front of his building and turned the little truck off; she jumped out right away.

She wasn't going to give him a chance to send her away. He was hurting, she knew it, and she knew she could make him feel better.

He strode past her without a word, and she followed him up the stairs. He unlocked the door to his loft and stood to let her enter first. So, even in his dark place, his manners were somewhat sticking around.

He closed the door behind him and headed for the kitchen. "You want a drink?"

She watched him go directly to the cupboard over the stove and pull down a half-empty bottle of Jack Daniels. He reached for a glass and Caitlyn was behind him. She covered his hand with hers and pressed her body against his side.

"You don't need a drink, Jack."

He stiffened. "You don't know what I need."

"Yes, I do. You need to remember how to feel, how to enjoy. How to live."

"You think I don't feel anything?" His eyes narrowed and he glared at her, pulling his hand out from under hers and grabbing the liquor bottle. "I feel too damn much, and sometimes the only thing that numbs it is my namesake."

She stood on tiptoe and brushed her lips across his before speaking softly, "Maybe you need to stop trying for numb. You need to move through it, let yourself feel everything. Just let yourself go."

"You want me to let myself go? What? You want me to break down and cry in your bosom, because there are some things in life I'd rather forget?"

"The 'men don't cry' mentality went out of style decades ago, Jack. But what I meant was to let go of it all, not just the sadness, but the anger, too."

His face hardened. "You don't know what you're talking about."

"So tell me." She ran a hand over his bunched chest muscles. "Tell me what it is that's got you tied up in knots so tight that you need to numb yourself with whiskey."

"I don't want to talk." He turned, clutching at her waist, his eyes glittering like cut emeralds. "Our deal wasn't that I go to the movie and we talk all night. I want to fuck."

His mouth came down on hers hard.

There was no gentleness as he parted her lips with his tongue and ravaged her mouth. He pushed her back against the counter and she wrapped her arms around him, letting him be rough, letting him take his anger and his pain out on her.

She opened herself up to him and let their energy blend with their breath. The taste of popcorn and Jack danced across her tongue and she shivered. His hands were fast and rough as they slid over her back and down to her butt.

He gripped her ass and pulled her tight to him, rocking against her in a way that let her feel every inch of his hardness through their clothes. Her body reacted, heating and softening, readying itself for him.

She lifted one leg and wrapped it around his hip, grinding against him, encouraging him to let loose, to feel everything between them. To accept what she was offering.

Her hands ran up his back, over the bunching and flexing muscles, and into his soft hair. The silky strands curled about her fingers and she sighed. He was the ultimate blend of soft and hard. Hard body, soft hair, hard attitude, soft lips . . .

One of his hands left her butt and ran up over her ribs under her shirt to cup a breast. He squeezed and she gasped; he scraped his teeth across her jaw and nipped at her neck and she whimpered. Heat followed everywhere he touched. Flames of desire that wouldn't be denied burned between them.

She needed more; she wanted to give him more.

She rocked her hips against him and the seam of her jeans pressed tight to her sex, rubbing and tantalizing, but it wasn't enough. He pulled down the neck of her top and sucked on her nipple through her bra, and her body jerked. "Jack . . ."

One hand fondled her breast while he sucked and bit at the nipple, the other slid between them and wrestled with her jeans. "Damn it," he growled, pulling back from her.

He grabbed her hand and pulled her over to the living area.

With a quick spin, he had her bent over the back of the sofa and her jeans down around her ankles. She gripped the edge of the couch, trying to steady her own breathing as the rasp of his zipper lowering echoed through the loft.

Then without any teasing or warning, he was between her legs, the head of his cock nudging at her entrance; she braced herself, only to feel his hands tighten on her hips.

"Cait?" His voice was harsh, raspy . . . unsure.

"Yes, Jack. Don't stop."

He let out a sharp breath, and within a split second, he filled her. There was no more hesitation as he thrust fast and hard. The sound of skin slapping against skin filled the room.

Cait's body bounced forward with each deep thrust, her breasts scraping against the rough fabric of the sofa. Jolts of pleasure went from her nipples to her core, and the knot of arousal deep in her belly grew, tightening with each slide of Jack's cock in and out of her body.

He pounded at her, grunting with each pump of his hips. Cait knew it was part passion and part pain, and she opened herself up to it all. Her insides tightened as pleasure swept over her and she cried out with it. Jack's shout of release blended with her cry, and his cock swelled and stretched her walls with his orgasm.

Cait relaxed against the sofa, her knees weak and her body pliant with satisfaction as her heartbeat started to slow. Jack stayed still, twitching inside her as he leaned forward and rested his head between her shoulders.

Jesus Christ, he was an asshole.

Jack tried desperately to get his heartbeat back under control. He'd lost it.

Cait had pushed a button and he'd lost it on her. Sure, she'd

222

said he could do anything, but somehow he didn't think the rough use she'd just endured was what she'd had in mind.

He'd had no right to use her that way, no matter what she'd said.

Unsure of exactly what to do next, he pulled out and zipped his pants. When she stayed bent over the sofa, he ran a rough hand through his hair and stared at her still form. God, he needed a drink. But first . . .

"Caitlyn?" He put a hand on her back and grimaced when she shivered in response.

She stirred, lifting her head and pushing back her tousled curls so he could see her face. Sleek brows drew together in a frown, and her eyes questioned him.

"You okay?"

She laughed and his gut clenched. It was a raw, husky laugh that hit him right in the chest and gave him hope. Her next words confirmed it.

"More than okay, Jack." She straightened up from the sofa and reached to pull up her jeans. Her cheeks were pink and her eyes were bright. She was almost . . . glowing or something. "That was one hell of an orgasm."

She came?

Shit, he'd been so wrapped up in his own battle between heaven and hell he hadn't even noticed! He did notice how her breasts bounced as she wiggled her way back into her jeans, though.

"Are you sure I didn't hurt you?"

She placed a warm hand on his cheek and brushed her lips against his. "I'm sure. I'm tougher than I look, Jack. And I did ask for it."

That she had.

He watched as she adjusted her bra and fixed her shirt.

"Why don't you just take it all off?" The words popped out of his mouth, surprising them both.

"You want me to stay?"

"I went to the movie, I get all night with you. That was the deal."

"Yes. Yes, it was." She smiled and his chest tightened. She reached for the snap on her jeans and began to push them back down her legs. "Your wish is my command for the rest of the night."

10

Jack shook his head.

What the hell had he ever done to deserve this woman barging into his life? His mind wasn't sure if she was welcome or not yet, but his body was all for her being there. By the time she'd shed her jeans and panties and pulled her shirt over her head, his cock was starting to show signs of life again.

Amazing.

He'd just emptied himself, and already he wanted her again. He stared at the bountiful flesh overflowing from the cups of some flimsy lace bra and his fingers tingled. He hadn't spent near enough time with those yet.

"Lose the bra, too," he said roughly.

She reached behind her back and undid it. She tossed it over the sofa and stood before him, naked, proud, and completely open.

"Follow me," he said, and headed for the bedroom.

"Yes, sir."

When he turned to look at her, she just winked playfully and scampered behind him. Tension flowed from him as he realized she was enjoying this. Not in a weird self-abusive type of way, but she really seemed to be happy to be with him. To please him even.

She was so completely open about *everything* she was feeling that he believed her earlier statement about not being easy for everyone. God help him, but there was something unique happening between them, and he was starting to think that maybe, just maybe, it would be good to have her hang around occasionally.

A chuckle rose in his chest and he let it out. Who was he to deny her if she wanted to come over and "play" with him?

He entered his bedroom and turned on the overhead light. He stripped as he watched her look around. She wandered over to his dresser and looked at the crap he had spread out on top of it. He watched her move to the far wall where he had some snapshots framed and hung.

"Is that you?" She pointed at a picture.

He didn't need to see it to know which one she was asking about. It was the one of two young boys standing in front of a snow fort they'd built. He ignored her question and the emotions that it raised. "Come on over here, babe."

His chest tightened when Caitlyn immediately spun around and moved to stand in front of him.

He studied her face, seeing the slight flush to her cheeks, the heat in her eyes. Her tongue darted out and slid across her bottom lip making it all shiny and pink.

He reached out and wrapped a hand around the back of her neck, bringing her closer. "I won't be so rough this time."

He kissed her, slowly and leisurely, enjoying the softness of her lips, the rasp of tongue against tongue. She pressed her body against him, her hands going around his back. He walked forward slowly, until she hit the bed; then he lowered her back onto it, covering her body with his.

How long had it been since he'd felt a woman beneath him? Heat flowed from her to him, it seeped through his skin and into his blood as he concentrated on her taste, her touch. On touching her.

He trailed his lips across her neck and sucked on her earlobe as he reached for one plump breast. The supple flesh overflowed his palm, but she practically purred at his touch. He tweaked the rigid nipple, tugged on the little ring there, and felt her body jerk.

"Okay?" he asked.

"Oh, yes," she purred.

He tugged on the ring again and her back arched. *Nice.* He reached for the other one and pulled it slowly until the nipple was stretched and she was panting loudly. Her hips pressed against him, rubbing and pressing. He could feel her excitement on his skin, like she was marking him or something.

He released his hold on the rings and soothed the nipples with his tongue. First one, then the other. Back and forth he laved, sucked, and nipped until her nails were digging into his back and her thighs were squeezing his hips.

Then he slid lower, rubbing his cheek against the softness of her belly, inhaling the scent of her arousal as it blended with the light, clean perfume she wore.

He kissed her belly, then slid his tongue over her smooth-shaven pubes to the hard little clit poking out the top of her slit. Her hips bucked and he slid his arms under her legs, his hands cupping her ass and lifting her, holding her still as he nuzzled his way between her swollen pussy lips. He licked her from one end to the other, stiffening his tongue and dipping it into her entrance.

He tasted his own muskiness mixed in with her flavor, and his cock thickened. She was his and only his.

He thrust his tongue in and out, rubbing his nose against her clit with each move. Her fingers tightened in his hair as her hips rolled, and her whimpers filled the room. He tightened his grip on her ass and shifted his focus. Dragging air in and out through his nose, his head filled with her scent as he locked his lips around her clit and sucked.

First, he was gentle and rhythmic, but as her cries got louder, he sucked a bit harder. He flicked it with his tongue and felt it swell and harden; then she pulled his hair, and juices covered his chin while she came.

Without stopping to let her rest, he drew up and thrust home. Her cunt was still spasming, and the hot wetness clutching at him nearly sent him over the edge. As it was, he locked his elbows and started to thrust slowly. He watched her as she arched into him, little white teeth clamped down on her bottom lip. She was so damn beautiful. Sweat gleamed on her skin and her hair was a mess, but her eyes were bright, and when she met his gaze, she grinned wickedly and raked her nails over his ass.

His hips bucked forward, burying himself deep inside her as tremors racked his body and fireworks went off behind his eyes.

He collapsed on top of her, enjoying the feel of her soft body full length against his for a minute before rolling off her to the side.

She curled against his side, kissing his chest softly. Jack threw an arm over his eyes while he sucked in air and wondered what the hell he was doing.

11

Caitlyn watched Jack sleep. His face was soft and his breathing deep. She'd inched away from him a few moments ago because his body was giving off enough heat to melt ice and she wasn't used to it.

He'd surprised her.

She hadn't expected the almost loving attention he'd shown in their go 'round. Well, she knew he'd be capable of it at some point, but with his high walls and hard attitude, she'd expected it to take a lot more time before he'd show anything close to tenderness. And there *had been* tenderness in his touch. Even if he wasn't aware of it.

She watched his chest rise and fall with his breathing and crept a little closer to him. The regret in his eyes after he'd fucked her in the living room had been hard to see. She didn't want him to ever regret being open and honest in his emotions around her, no matter what those emotions were. Besides that, she wasn't a small, fragile female; his passion had enflamed her, not hurt her.

She crawled from the bed and turned off the light before

lying down again. Unsure of what to expect next, she reached out and placed her hand over his heart, rested a leg along the length of his, and closed her eyes.

She was staying with him for as long as she could.

Jack came awake with the crystal clarity that he wasn't alone. Caitlyn wasn't touching him, and his first instinct was to reach out for her. Then his brain woke up and stopped him.

He laid there a few minutes, silent and still, her presence beside him a warm, seductive thing. It was both comforting and disturbing.

No sun peaked in between the curtains, which meant it was still dark out. He glanced at the clock on the nightstand. Four-thirty in the morning.

Without looking to see if Caitlyn was awake or not, he got off the bed and stepped into his jeans. He padded barefoot from the room while pulling a T-shirt over his head. Restless energy pumped through his body; there was no way he'd be able to go back to sleep. His mind was wide-awake with memories, and his body was humming with sexual need.

He could bury himself in Caitlyn again. Hide from himself inside her and the warm blanket of sensations she brought on with every touch. He truly was insatiable when it came to her. But for some reason, the craving for numbness, the urge to forget, they were fading.

Not wanting to think about what was going on inside himself, Jack headed for his work area looking for a distraction.

12

When Caitlyn woke up the next morning, she was alone. Waking up alone in a strange bed would make most people feel a bit freaked out, but she was okay with it. The loft was silent, and sunlight was visible between the crack in the heavy curtains. She stretched on the bed, welcoming the delicious soreness of a well-used body.

She got up and pulled on her blouse; it was long and loose enough to cover everything it needed to, if a little see through without her bra on. Not that it mattered, she wasn't shy, especially with Jack.

She padded out of the bedroom in search of the bathroom. She used the toilet and washed her hands and face. Spreading some toothpaste on her finger, she took care of her teeth and went in search of Jack.

As soon as she turned the corner into the open area she saw him in the corner with his drop cloths and work stuff. He didn't look up from whatever he was photographing, so she went into the kitchen to grab herself some of the coffee she could smell.

Full mug in hand, she strolled over to his work area and

leaned against the table by the wall. The same one she'd sat on for him the other day.

"Morning," she said softly.

"Good morning," he replied. He straightened up and she saw what he was working on.

"A bowl of fruit salad?" She raised her eyebrows.

His lips tilted and he nodded. "Pictures for the menu of some restaurant. Boring, but it pays the bills."

Caitlyn nodded. He looked better this morning. His aura was still shady, but not so much the dark cloud it was the day she met him. His eyes ran over her from head to toe, lingering on her breasts and bare legs. Green fire leapt to life in his gaze, and she responded. Her nipples stiffened and her insides melted.

Not speaking, he walked toward her, reached behind her without breaking eye contact, and stepped back with another camera in his hand.

She didn't move, instinct telling her that something important was happening.

Jack raised the camera to his eye and started taking pictures of her. He moved slowly, from one side to the other, bending a little, changing the camera angle.

Neither of them spoke, but she watched him the whole time, staring into the camera and not moving except to cock her head to the side and follow his movements.

When he'd snapped a dozen pictures and showed no sign of stopping, she clued into something. He was a photographer. A man who made his living looking through a camera, and she bet he saw things a lot more clearly through a lens that he ever did with the naked eye.

Words didn't mean a lot to this man. What he saw did. Actions did.

With that in mind, she put down her coffee mug and started

to pose. She smiled into the camera, letting him see her happiness at being there with him. She could feel the air between them shift, Jack becoming more intent on her.

She spread her legs slightly and pulled her shirt down locking her elbows and giving him a little girl look. Then with a wicked grin, she tugged at the neckline as if she was going to flash him.

"That's it, baby. Flirt with the camera."

"I'm not flirting with the camera, sexy. I'm flirting with you." She turned sideways and struck a classic pinup pose.

"With me, huh? In that case, stop being so shy." There was a hint of laughter in his voice and Caitlyn's spirit soared.

A laugh bubbled up and out of her. "Me? Shy?"

She put a fingertip to her mouth and pouted. When he just chuckled and kept snapping shots, she went with it. She rimmed her nipples through her shirt, then turned and leaned on the table so that the bottom of her butt cheeks flashed beneath the hem of her shirt while she looked over her shoulder at him. She laughed and taunted and teased him.

"Such a bad girl you are," he said when he finally put the camera down.

He stood close to her, trapping her against the table, a finger running up and down her arm. "Here I thought you might get naked for me again, but you just tease and tease and tease."

His green eyes sparkled and she laughed up at him. "But you like the way I tease, don't ya?"

He growled and pressed closer, not touching, but close enough that the air between them heated. She was tempted, oh so tempted to let him just seduce her right out of her clothes, but she knew if she ever wanted them to have more than just sex between them, she had to shift gears.

She placed a hand flat on his chest and stopped him from

coming any closer. "I'm not teasing with my offer to cook breakfast, though. You hungry?" She raised an eyebrow at him, keeping a smile on her lips and her gaze locked with his.

His eyes narrowed and his gaze sharpened. But it didn't dull, and for that she was glad. "I could eat," he said.

She leaned forward and placed a quick kiss on his mouth before sauntering to the kitchen.

13

Jack listened to Caitlyn moving around in the kitchen. It had been a long time since he'd heard the sounds of someone else in his home. Shit, he'd never even really thought of the loft as a home before. It was just where he slept.

Caitlyn had turned on the radio and was singing along with it. He tried to concentrate on the job at hand, emptying the cameras and labeling the film canisters.

He needed to get the menu photos in to his client in a couple days, and the urge to step into his dark room and develop the roll of Caitlyn was almost overwhelming.

She'd looked so warm and rumpled when she'd been standing there that he'd had to capture the image, the memory.

He stared out the loft window at nothing. He hadn't taken a photograph for the pure want of doing it since he'd returned from South America. Even before that, if he really thought about it.

"Breakfast is served."

Jack started, coming back to the present with a thump. He debated walking away from Caitlyn. Going to take a shower or simply crawl back into bed and wait until she left. She was going to leave anyway; she'd just wanted a good time, and she'd gotten it.

"Jack?" Her hand landed on his shoulder. "Are you okay?"

"Of course." He shrugged her off and headed for the kitchen. He had to eat sometime, it may as well be now.

He pulled up a seat at the table and waited for her to sit across from him before digging in.

There was silence for the first few minutes; then she started to ask questions.

"You want to tell me about it?"

"About what?"

"About what made you shut down."

His heart pounding, he looked at her. "What do you mean?"

She sat back and considered him. He could almost see the gears grinding in her head. Then she made a decision. "You were obviously emotionally wounded at some point in the past. Something that hurt you bad enough that you gave up a career I hear you were heading for the top of, to do . . . this." She waved her hand toward the studio corner.

Friends had asked him about why he'd dumped his career two years ago. His family had asked him. He'd just shaken their questions off with the standard line, "It was time for a change." He'd even believed it.

But the memories that haunted him, the lack of sleep. Shit, the movie they'd seen last night and even the way she'd picked up on the photo in his room . . . He couldn't lie anymore. Not even to himself.

"Shut down," he muttered. "That's an . . . apt description."

"The first time I saw you, I knew you were hurting—not physically so much as spiritually and emotionally."

"Yeah? Is that why you gave me a sex show? Because my

spirit was damaged?" Damn, it was a bit harder to talk than he'd thought.

Her eyes flashed, but other than that, she didn't react to his barb. "I also knew that I could help you. That I wanted to help you."

The urge to talk fled, and he pushed his half-empty plate aside. So he was a pity fuck now? "Thanks, anyway, but I don't need your help. Life happened and I decided a change was needed. It's not a big deal."

"Jack—"

"I got everything I needed from you last night, babe. A couple of orgasms to soothe the savage beast, and I'm good to go." He stared her down. "You should go, too."

"I know you used to be a top photojournalist, Jack. I know you're a smart man with talent, and I think you used to have some drive, too. So what happened?" The stubborn wench sat back in her chair and eyed him pointedly. "What happened to make you shut down and hide like a whipped dog?"

"Fuck that!" He stood up fast, knocking over his chair. He glared at her, panic and pain exploding in his chest. His hands curled into fists and he strode out of the kitchen.

He stomped into the living area and heard her chair scrape across the floor and her footsteps follow. Fuckin' woman, why wouldn't she just leave him alone?

"I'm not going to let you just walk away from this, Jack. I'm not going to let you just push me out the door and out of your life."

"Why not? Why the hell would you even want to be part of my life? What makes you think it's so great? I'm sure you can find plenty of men who would be happy to rock your world."

She crossed her arms over her chest and gazed at him. "You're right, I can. Finding a man has never been a problem for me. Finding the *right man* has been, though. And I think you're the right one."

He snorted out loud and turned his back on her to cover up the shock he felt. Joy had washed over him at her declaration, and he was having a hard time with it.

"Why is it so hard for you to believe, Jack?"

He turned back to her. "You reading my mind now?"

"You're not that hard to read, you know."

He remembered what Teal had said about the whole headache thing and he frowned. "Oh yeah, you're psychic or something, right?"

Caitlyn hesitated. She'd never been afraid to explain her abilities to people before. She was who she was, and she wouldn't apologize for it. But she knew opening up to Jack when he was ready to lash out could hurt.

She also knew that if she really did believe he was the one for her, she couldn't hide anything from him.

"I'm not psychic. I can see auras and manipulate a person's energy to help balance them, to heal them."

His gaze snapped fire as he laughed mockingly. "So you fucked me because you wanted to heal me? That's rich."

Wrapping her arms tighter around herself, she worked to hold in her own pain. He was just lashing out because he was hurting. For whatever reason, he didn't *want* to care.

"Actually, yes. To me, sexual energy is the purest, so it would make sense it would have the strongest effect on you." His eyes widened, then narrowed dangerously as he stalked forward. She held up her hand before he could say something he might really regret. "And, no, I don't have to have sex to heal people. I wanted to do it with you because . . ."

"Because what?" he growled.

"Because you're special. Don't shake your head at me, Jack. You can't deny that from the first minute we met there was an attraction. There was chemistry and I could feel your energy reaching out to me. You needed me, and I wanted to be there for you. I still want to be there for you. Not just because I think I can help you arrive at some sort of peace for whatever it was that hurt you so bad, but because *I like you.*"

She stepped forward and pressed her hands against his hard chest. "I like your intelligence, even your sarcasm. I like your ability to see things that aren't clear to everyone, like the sheik and harem thing with the chain. You're on the same wavelength as me. Our energies balance each other naturally. That's why I could sense your distress in the movie theater without even looking at you. It's also why you feel better when I'm around. We balance each other out, Jack. We fit. And if you give it— give *us*—half a chance, we could have something special."

Cait looked up into Jack's piercing green eyes and saw the answer before he even spoke. His walls were up and he'd locked himself away deep inside. He wasn't even radiating anger anymore. He was simply . . . there.

He stepped back and shook his head, not meeting her gaze. "You should go now."

Claws reached deep into her chest and squeezed her heart. "Jack, I'm not pushing you for me . . . I'm doing it for you. Don't you want to find some peace? Some happiness?"

"With you? Who says I'm not happy now? Doesn't my aura tell you I just want to be left alone?"

This time he looked right at her, and the emotionlessness of his gaze hurt more than his avoidance. "I would like it to be with me, but if not . . . then for yourself. Tell me what it is in your past so you can heal, and I'll leave you alone to do it."

"You want to know? Fine. A couple of years ago, my childhood friend, who'd joined the army to get an education and stayed because he believed in being a peacekeeper, ended up dead in a 'friendly fire' accident in the Middle East." His bitterness was clear as he continued, and her heart ached for him. "There's no such thing as *friendly fire*. Why the hell they think that's a good term to use I'll never know."

"I'm sorry, Jack. It was the boy in the picture with you, wasn't it?"

He nodded. "Yup. You know, it wasn't so much that he died. I mean, I hate that he died, and I hate that he died that way, but in his letters before that, I could tell that he was having trouble with what they were doing over there. He felt they weren't doing everything they could, or even enough to make a difference. So when he was killed, I asked to be sent over to work on a story."

He started to pace the room and Caitlyn watched as his energy shifted. He was upset but calm. The tendrils of darkness she'd seen in his aura that first day were almost gone.

"When I got there, everything was great. All the soldiers put on a brave face for me. . . . but the longer I stayed, the more I could see that it was an act. Almost each and every one of them were frustrated and pissed off at the government for not doing what it could. For not letting them do what *they* could because of politics. We saw devastated villages and women clutching their children tight with terror on their faces whenever they saw us. It didn't matter that we were a battalion of peacekeepers. We were foreign men, in uniform, with guns. And we weren't wanted."

Caitlyn didn't know what to say. There was nothing she could say that would make it all right. Instead, she listened.

"So I left. I left the war and the peacekeeping behind, and took an assignment in South America for a travel magazine. It was supposed to be a fluff piece on the best beaches. Pretty places for people to visit. Only it seemed like everything below the surface there was rotten, too. There were guerillas camped just outside the cities, and kidnapping tourists was a money-making industry for them. The local governments left the kidnappers and drug lords alone because they had their own wars to fight."

"It just seems like everywhere I turn now I see ugliness. Like there is no real good out there in the world."

Sympathy was good, she felt for Jack, but she could see the darkness coming back. The depression, the hopelessness. She needed to remind him that life went on, and it really was what you made of it. "So you decided to spend the rest of your life taking pictures of fruit salad?"

His head snapped around, anger flashing in his eyes. But he didn't say anything.

"Bad things happen all the time, Jack. But good things do, too. You can't have one without the other, and if you stay holed up in here, you're not going to have either of them."

"Don't go giving me a speech on how life is for living and it's all what I make of it. Jared tried to make life good for a lot of people, and what did it do for him? Nothing. That's what."

"Jack—"

"No, don't! I get that you think you can heal people. And you know what? A good fuck every now and then is always welcome, but I don't need healing." His voice was as hard as his gaze. "I just need to be left alone."

14

Jack's head was swimming and his chest was tight. How could this be happening? Really? A woman who thinks she can heal him through sex? Who even said he needed healing? He'd been doing just fine on his own.

Yeah, keep telling yourself that, buddy. Maybe you'll start to believe it.

He paced the loft, fighting the urge to go after Caitlyn. He knew he'd hurt her. When she'd dressed and left, she'd hidden it well, but he could tell. Her stiff shoulders, her silence. All the warmth he naturally associated with her was gone.

He didn't like that he'd hurt her feelings, but it wasn't really his problem. He didn't ask her to care. Hell, he'd never asked her for anything. He was doing fine before she'd showed up at his door. Then she'd invited herself into his life, and in the space of twenty-four hours, she'd turned him inside out. How could she possibly expect him to welcome that?

Healing through sex. Yeah, right.

15

"I'm gonna hurt him. That jackass needs to suffer!"

Caitlyn stayed still, frozen on Mia's sofa where she'd fallen asleep after crying on her best friend's shoulder while they drank a bottle of wine.

She could hear Mia clearly ranting in the kitchen and part of her wanted to go in there and assure her friend she'd be fine, but when she moved, she was reminded that Mia hadn't really drank any of the wine. It had all been her.

"Shhh, baby. It's all right. Caitlyn is going to be fine." Dominick's voice was soothing. He'd learned well in a short time how to deal with Mia's quick temper.

"How could he just brush her off like that, Dom? You said this guy was a good man. Caitlyn has such a good heart. She only ever wants to help people, and she deserves better than to be fucked over like this."

Dom's response was muffled, and then so was Mia's. Caitlyn closed her eyes and buried her face into the sofa cushion. She'd wandered around the city for a while after leaving Jack's and had ended up back at Mia's. It had been one in the afternoon when she'd started drinking, and she didn't have a clue what time it was when she'd woken up, but she wasn't moving until the room stopped spinning.

Jack's rejection had hurt. It shouldn't have hurt so much. Not when she'd only known him so short a time. They'd talked with their bodies way more than they had with words. She hated to admit it, but as much as she wanted to think she knew him, she didn't.

She had plenty of opinions, ideas, and instinct, but very little real knowledge.

Tears welled behind her eyes and she concentrated on her breathing. Opening her heart, she focused on the soft murmur of her friends' voices and drifted back into the welcoming darkness.

A week later, Caitlyn was standing outside Lush chewing on her bottom lip. Teal and Zach's official engagement party was in full swing inside the gallery and she wasn't sure she could force herself to go in.

She hadn't heard from Jack, and she hadn't reached out to him, either. It had been hard. She still believed deep down that he was the one for her—the yang to her ying. But she wasn't ready to go back to him for another emotional beating.

She'd rushed things with him, and she was paying the price. Sure, he'd shared himself with her. But then he'd slammed the door in her face and she wasn't sure he'd ever open the door to her again.

A burst of laughter sounded inside the gallery and she squared her shoulders. She wasn't going to stand out there like a loser when her friends were inside celebrating. She was strong, she was tough . . . and she wasn't scared of the fact that Jack might be inside.

Breathing slowly and deeply, she pulled the door open and stepped inside.

"Caitlyn! You made it after all!" Mia rushed over and Caitlyn drank in the love when she was wrapped in her friend's arms. "He's here."

Mia's whisper sent a shiver down her spine. She pulled back and met her friend's concerned gaze.

"He is, huh?" Caitlyn smiled. "It's okay. I've made a decision about him and I'm ready to stand firm."

"Really?" Mia's eyebrows jumped. "Care to tell me what it is?"

"Not until I tell him."

Mia's eyes narrowed and Caitlyn laughed. "It's all right, sister. I'm good."

"In that case, let's get you a drink." Mia snagged a glass of wine from a passing waiter and handed it to Caitlyn. Caitlyn put it to her lips and pretended to drink. It would be a while before she was ready to indulge again. Hangovers were not her favorite thing, and even a week later, the last one still messed with her ability to give a good massage.

Caitlyn glanced around the crowded gallery and saw Teal and Zach, arm in arm as they chatted with an older couple. There was a bright yellow aura around the whole group, with tinges of purple and blue. Lots of love and happiness in that group.

She saw Dominick chatting animatedly with a tall, lanky blond guy with arms covered in tattoos. There were people she didn't know milling around, and she tried not to be obvious in her search for Jack. She was surprised he was there.

Pleasantly surprised, though, because it could mean that he'd decided it was time to get out of his loft just a bit. She looked at some of the displays as she wandered and stopped dead in front of Mia's jewelry.

The line was simply titled *Mia.* Each decoration was mounted onto a black card with a shaded image behind it. Caitlyn recognized herself in the shaded images, but she doubted anyone else would. The nipple piercings had a picture of her fingertip playing with her own barbell. The waist chains had the image of her waist on it, looking soft and feminine, but ultimately sexy and erotic.

There were earrings, finger rings, and toe rings. There were even ankle bracelets, with the photos of her behind them. But it was the big photo mounted on the wall behind the display that really shocked her. How she'd missed it when she first walked in she didn't know.

It was all her. Completely naked, she lounged on the pillows, hair spread out, eyelids at half-mast as she looked into the camera with seductive promise.

One knee was bent at an angle so that her leg hid the hand that was tucked between her thighs. The other hand was curled under her chin.

There was an amazing combination of innocence and allure to the photo that made her breath catch in her throat.

"Beautiful, isn't she?"

Her heart pounded at the husky voice near her ear.

Jack.

16

Would she talk to him? He'd felt her stiffen and knew she recognized his voice. *Come on, Caitlyn. Talk to me.*

"She's the most beautiful thing I've ever seen," he said again.

Caitlyn turned to him, her eyes wide. His heart pounded in his chest, and sweat broke out all over his body.

"Then why did you chase her away?"

He swallowed. "I was an idiot. An asshole. I didn't know a good thing when it was staring me in the face."

"Do you know now?"

"Yes." He reached for her hand, grateful when she let him hold it. "I do."

"Jack." She shook her head.

"Caitlyn, I'm sorry. Things just happened too damn fast, and I panicked."

"Jack—"

"I want another chance." He interrupted her. He wouldn't give her a chance to tell him off. Not until after he had his say. "I want to try. I can't make any promises. I can be a real bastard, and I doubt it's going to change overnight. But you were right. I feel like shit, and . . . Well, I don't feel that way when you're around. When you're with me I start to believe there is still beauty in the world, and I need that." He took a deep breath. "I need you."

She stepped back, her eyes hidden from him behind her curls as she tilted her head and gazed at him.

"You need me, huh?"

Shit. He barely kept himself from grabbing her hands to stop her from stepping away from him. "I'm sorry I can't give you a pretty speech full of promises of love and happily ever after. I can be a bastard, I know that. But I'm honest, and I'm trying to change. You made me want to change. I want to give this—give *us* a chance."

Her eyes ran over his face and he knew right then that if she denied him, he'd find another way to see her again. He wasn't a complete idiot; he wasn't going to let her walk away from him, even if he'd been the one to tell her to go before.

His gut clenched and he girded himself for her rejection when a sparkle bloomed in her eye, her lips split into a grin, and she threw her arms around him.

"I wasn't going to let you get away, you know," she said into his ear. He wrapped his arms around her and buried his face in her neck. Her scent warmed him as he held his precious package so tight he was scared he'd hurt her as her whispered words massaged the numbness from his heart. "I was just giving you a bit of time before I came over to see if you wanted to play again."

Meet three men with something extra—a supernatural, fierce sensuality that transforms them into lovers like no others. For the women who love them, the call of the wild cannot be denied . . .

FALLEN by Kate Douglas

With secret powers that intensify their senses, master shapeshifters Mik and AJ are on the prowl in New Mexico, seeking to rescue a lost kin named Tala, a woman sold into bondage and desperate to escape. Free of her captors, Tala will experience true liberation with Mik and AJ—an uninhibited *ménage a trois* that takes her to the heights of erotic pleasure and reveals her true Chanku nature . . .

FANTAISIE by Noelle Mack

Brought to a French chateau wreathed in mist, at once elegant and eerie, Tanya meets a mysterious man whose wild mane of hair and golden eyes are like nothing she has ever seen. Though Jean Claude keeps as guardian a lion that is anything but tame, she is free to explore the chateau's many rooms, where mirages appear of lovers who once satisfied their deepest desires there. Jean Claude is among them—but is his current incarnation something other than human? Tanya cannot resist the erotic spell in his eyes . . .

CALL OF THE WILD by Kathleen Dante

Knowing nothing of the wolf clan whose blood she shares, Deanna Lycan is strangely drawn to all things wild—and compelled to begin a sensual exploration of her true nature with Graeme Luger. Their torrid encounter sweeps her toward a transformation that will bring her to the ultimate ecstasy . . .

Please turn the page for an exciting sneak peek of Kathleen Dante's *Call of the Wild* now on sale in SEXY BEAST II!

1

Shifting to a lower gear, Deanna Lycan took yet another S-curve in the endless mountains with more caution than was her wont. Laden with all her worldly belongings, her sporty CR-V was less nimble than usual, and she didn't want to push it.

Anyway, there was no rush. No one was expecting her. No one would mind if she got to Hillsboro tomorrow or next week instead of today. She stifled the familiar pang of loneliness the thought evoked. That might change, if her inquiries proved fruitful. She could only hope she wasn't off on a fool's quest.

Few vehicles shared the winding two-lane highway, allowing her to snatch an occasional glance at the scenery.

On one side was a steep mountain covered by hardwood and pines, but the other side was a drop-off that plunged to a rushing stream hundreds of feet below. Every few turns revealed another breathtaking vista of blue mountains stretching rank upon rank into the distance, seemingly untouched by the summer heat.

The sight of all that open space soothed something inside her, calming the restlessness that for the past year had made her miserable in Boston. A strange development for the city girl she knew herself to be. But she couldn't deny the sense of homecoming she felt at seeing the panorama, after nearly a decade since she'd last beheld its like.

The endless double yellow lines unrolled along the middle of the road before her, faithfully snaking along the curves, dividing the narrow highway into equal lanes. Rather like the way her future had looked before she'd decided to pull up stakes. Steady, static, sterile . . . and ultimately stifling.

Who would have thought that Boston with its picturesque neighborhoods echoing with history and its concerts and plays and museums—cultural activities she enjoyed—would now encroach on her?

Too little room, too many people, too many strangers—and no family.

Suddenly, it had been like she couldn't breathe.

It had gotten so bad that she hadn't allowed a man in her bed in months. Couldn't stand the thought of sharing her space.

Well, hopefully, all that would change in Hillsboro. And she was taking the first step toward making it happen.

Deanna made a face. Jump-start her dismal love life? Who was she kidding? Just because she was relocating didn't mean she'd find someone who'd awaken her dormant libido. Which was a pity since the horizontal tango used to be a lot of fun.

She took a tight turn and hard plastic rattled in the backseat, maybe her measuring cups. Since whatever it was sounded loose, not broken, she ignored it.

Except for that, the humming of the CR-V's tires filled the silence. She'd turned off the radio sometime back, after the mountains started interfering with reception. The cell phone in her purse was just as quiet, which was fine with her.

She'd put everything on hold. All her clients knew she was

on vacation—her first in years. Anyway, it wasn't as if web design generated that many emergency calls.

Hoping for a whiff of green, Deanna lowered her window to let the wind play through her hair, making the wavy locks dance across her shoulders, and angled her body so the breeze blew down the front of her tank top. Despite being on a highway, there was barely a hint of exhaust fumes in the flow of warm air that caressed her body, a welcome contrast to urban smog.

The next turn unveiled another panorama of mountains and clear sky, an infinite palette of blues she couldn't hope to capture in her designs. If it weren't for the wide steel guardrail, it could have been the same sight first beheld centuries past by the colonists who'd settled the area.

She smiled at the romantic notion. That's what came from knowing nothing of her ancestry: trying to connect with some history greater than her own. Growing up in an orphanage, knowing nothing much about her parents, save that they'd died in a car accident when she was four, had given her a thirst for heritage. Deep roots. But, somehow, she didn't think anything she might learn about her parents could live up to such fantastic pipe dreams.

A loud, protesting *BLAT!* from behind broke the tranquil afternoon drive.

She shot a glance at the rearview mirror and stared.

Reflected there, a black pickup swerved onto the highway, cutting in with utter disregard for traffic and safety. To her dismay, it was speeding up as it weaved unsteadily between lanes, repeatedly crossing the double yellow lines and gaining on her.

Deanna forced her attention back to the road in front. It would do her little good to avoid the danger behind her, only to drive off the highway or get into a crash herself.

The road curved away from the mountainside onto a short viaduct that cut across a narrow valley. In the straightaway, she opened the throttle, coaxing more speed from her faithful CR-V, her heart in her throat, the steering wheel biting into her white-knuckled hands. Behind her, the roar came on like an unstoppable nightmare, loud and getting louder.

BEEEEEP!

The car behind her fishtailed across the road as its driver lost control, leaving nothing between her and the weaving pickup.

No matter how hard she looked, there was nowhere she could turn off to let the truck behind her pass, and no cops when she needed one. She could only stay ahead or hope its driver came to his senses.

The uneven race continued off the viaduct and back on another mountainside, the truck rapidly making up the distance between it and her car.

Deanna stomped down on the accelerator. The CR-V responded sluggishly, weighed down by her belongings. Plastic rattled, the disparate odors of cinnamon, paprika, and fennel swirling through the car. Her spice rack must have fallen over.

The road twisted once more, another picturesque valley unfolding to her right. But she didn't have time to appreciate its beauty or to wish away another metal guardrail so rooted in the modern day.

Veering across the double yellow lines again, the black pickup charged on with the roar of a revving engine.

Time seemed to stop. All sounds vanished as if nature held its breath.

As Deanna watched with horror, the truck's silver grille and massive bull-bar glinted in the afternoon sun, headed straight at her.

THUNK!

The door slammed into Deanna's side, a scarlet starburst of pain that drove the breath from her lungs.

Tires squealed.

The CR-V slid toward the shoulder, gravel pinging on its undercarriage. Another impact threw her in the opposite direction, to land on top of her bulky purse. There was a long screech, like the wailing of the damned, as her faithful car jounced around her.

Another metal shriek filled the air, then silence.

For a long moment, the world stood still. Then the bottom dropped, dragging Deanna with it.

On most days, Graeme Luger enjoyed his job as a sheriff deputy in Woodrose, West Virginia. The town was perfect for his needs. It gave him a forest to run wild in, good people worthy of protection, relatively quick access to clan with a few hours' drive—and a steady stream of potential mates in the form of hikers and other tourists. Not that he'd had any success to date, but there was always tomorrow.

Today, however, didn't look to be one of the good days.

Pulling onto the gravelly shoulder, he parked behind another patrol car and took in the situation with a quick glance, noting skid marks, the broken guardrail, and the black pickup opposite laying on its side up the mountain. Several vehicles were abandoned in disarray along the grassy verge, their erstwhile drivers crowding the edge of the road.

His lips twisted in an automatic snarl at the sight.

Henckel again. He ran a hand through his wiry crew cut. If he weren't prematurely gray already, the scene would have given him white hairs. This time the sheriff couldn't turn a blind eye to the young drunk's shenanigans. *Go straight to jail. Do not pass GO. Do not collect two hundred dollars.* Just because Henckel had led the high school football team to state victory was no excuse for this.

The prospect would have cheered him if it weren't for the cost. It shouldn't have been permitted to get this far.

Getting out of his patrol car, Graeme hotfooted over to join his fellow deputy by the guardrail, weaving through the rubber-neckers crowding the narrow shoulder.

"Gray!" The audible relief in Mitchell's voice made his gut tense.

"Henckel?"

"Over there. He'll keep." The older man jerked his chin at the fallen pickup. "More's the pity," he added in a mutter that Graeme's sharp ears caught.

"This one won't." Mitchell pointed downhill through the break in the guardrail as Graeme reached his side.

On a small ridge nearly a hundred feet below, a battered gold Honda CR-V was snagged on a young pine that was bending under the strain. Its driver—a woman—was bashing at the windshield, crazed, clawing shattered glass clear of the frame, not waiting to be rescued. The massive dent on the driver's door and streaks of black gouged on its paint said Henckel's truck had rammed the car. The damage must have jammed the door.

Graeme reined in the flicker of admiration he felt at her initiative, knowing he probably didn't have much time. Even in the brief seconds he'd taken to study the situation, the car had slipped noticeably. It was up to him to save that woman.

Grant Mitchell was a good man to have at his back, but agile was the last word anybody would use to describe him. Short with most of his weight carried in a thick potbelly, the other deputy wasn't one for scrambling down mountainsides. He left that to the younger guys like Graeme, who was in far better shape, and contented himself with providing support.

As he did now, bellowing at the crowd to stand aside and clearing the way for Graeme to sprint back to his patrol car.

Popping the trunk, Graeme snatched up the climbing gear he kept there for similar emergencies. He raced back, rope slung over his shoulder. No time for anything fancy. Every second counted, as the tortured creaking from below attested. He wound the rope around a bent guardrail, tied it off on a nearby bumper, then started down the steep slope. The post creaked under his weight but held. Dislodged by his hasty passage, a minor avalanche of hard soil accompanied his rapid descent, clattering fit to startle wildlife.

Adrenaline had his heart pounding, sharpening his awareness until he could pick out the pungent bite of crushed wildflowers, the sour sweat of the milling rubberneckers, and the nauseatingly sweet stench of hot rubber from forty feet away, even in his human form.

Graeme had to pause to shake his head clear. Times like this, his heightened werewolf senses were a danger on the job.

An updraft of warm air brought him the scent of flowing sap and something else that raised his hackles and—inexplicably— set his cock twitching. What a damned inconvenient time for his hunting instinct to raise its head! He ignored his reaction, focusing his attention on getting down to the trapped driver. If he wanted to save her, he couldn't afford any distraction.

As he continued down the sharp incline, he passed broken trees scarred with gold paint. Marked by the Honda's passage, they must have slowed its fall, which probably explained the driver's good condition.

At the top of the ridge, Graeme released the rope and turned to the battered car. His heart skipped at the lack of motion that met him. The woman had stopped trying to clear the windshield. All he could see of her was light brown hair. Had she passed out?

To make matters worse, the pine groaned, an audible warning of impending failure.

Brushing aside the remains of the shattered glass still clinging to the frame, he tried to get a better look at the driver and assess the situation.

Her head snapped up, revealing startled hazel eyes.

Relief washed over him at her reaction. "Come on!" He stuck an arm through the hole in the windshield to help her out.

"I can't. The seatbelt's jammed!" She'd twisted out from under the diagonal chest strap, but the lap band kept her trapped. A few frayed threads bore testament to her efforts at cutting the seatbelt.

And he could barely reach it from where he stood.

He'd have to go through the window.

Taking a deep breath, Graeme braced his hands on the twisted metal.

A stirring perfume fogged his senses. It set his cock springing to steel-hard awareness and made his shoulders bunch with instinctive aggression that bypassed intellectual control. The scent honed his temper to razor edge, outrage flaring in his heart. How dare Henckel endanger this woman!

Gripping the two sides of the window frame, he pushed, drawing on his werewolf strength to bend the steel to his will. It bit into his palms, resisting his efforts. But slowly, with shrill creaks of protest, the metal gave way.

As if in sympathy, the tree groaned.

The woman squeaked as the car shuddered around her.

Finally, there was enough space for him to fit.

"Let me at it." Leaning forward, Graeme managed to wedge his head and shoulders inside and grab the strap. The position blocked her view of his hands, but it nearly stuffed his face between a damned fine pair of knockers and nose deep in female ambrosia that next to short-circuited his wolf brain.

Her! That mouthwatering, blood-hailing scent was hers! Only long training kept him from howling. But, damn, she smelled oh so good.

"Sorry about this." His apology was muffled by the high mounds, but she must have heard him; at least she didn't slap his mug while he worked at freeing her.

Confident his hands were hidden, he changed one, a tingle of heat flooding it as his finger contracted and claws emerged. He slashed down, the band parting easily with a brief rip.

He bumped his head on the frame as he jerked back, the jarring contact little more than a distraction. "Come on."

Pushing a large purse ahead of her, the busty brunette scrambled out of her seat, one hand clutching his biceps as she squeezed through the window.

Wrapping an arm around her waist, Graeme secured her to his chest, one unprofessional corner of his brain registering the soft breasts plumped against him. Gripping her *firm, round ass* with his other hand, he yanked her clear, scrambling backward as the ground shook.

And not a moment too soon.

As he set her on her feet, a loud *crack* announced the tree's demise. With the loss of its support, the car slid off the ridge, tumbling down the steep ravine.

"Oh, God!" Deanna clung to her rescuer, chilled by her close call. If it hadn't been for him, she'd still be trapped and might have accompanied her car even further down the mountain. She pressed closer to him, craving safety. Still feeling unsteady, she wrapped her legs around his, anchoring herself against the fear that threatened to shake her apart.

He stroked her back, crooning wordlessly; his gruff voice was reaching deep inside her, enfolding her in reassurance, and his big body a shield against the horror of her brush with death.

It had been a near thing.

Shivering with an uncharacteristic craving for support, she buried her face in his solid chest, soaking in the aura of strength that he radiated. The scent of fabric softener, sweat, and male filled her nose, calling to her like precious perfume.

Her empty sheath clenched, raw need coiled in her belly, sudden and unexpected. Unbidden and almost unfamiliar, it pinned her in place with a spine-tingling, knee-melting intensity that banished all thought. It had been months since she'd felt arousal, and never with such carnal violence.

Her rescuer wasn't immune to it either. His erection surged against her belly, swelling to an undeniable ridge, hard and thick with promise. All male hunger she wanted inside her.

Breathless with sensual awareness, Deanna stared up at him, into blue eyes gone silvery with desire. She clutched his belt, wanting to undo it, to release the turgid flesh caught between them. To take his cock into her wet pussy and ride him to blissful exhaustion. Her thighs practically quivered with need.

Her breasts tingled and firmed; her nipples poked through her thin bra and tank top. She wanted his mouth on them, sucking them, nibbling them until they ached. Her core pulsed with the strength of her desire.

"Gray!" The distant yell shattered the breathless moment.

Taking a deep breath, her rescuer turned his grizzled head to the shout. "We're coming!"

If only!

SEXY DEVIL
A two-story paranormal anthology from Sasha White
Coming soon from Aphrodisia!
An excerpt from the first story,
THE DEVIL INSIDE

Prologue

She couldn't look away.

He had her wrists pinned to the bed beside her head and his eyes locked on hers. His hips forward and he slid gently into her body. Her pulse raced and her legs wrapped around his waist, holding him tight to her. His rhythm picked up speed and she whimpered, her sex tightening around him, her body trembling with the strength of her approaching orgasm. Her heavy eyelids drooped, but she couldn't let them fall, couldn't look away from the well of emotions overflowing from his eyes.

"I love you, Gina," he whispered.

Joy filled her and she cried out, every muscle in her body taut as she squeezed him between her thighs. She squeezed harder and thrust her hips again. And felt nothing but emptiness. He was gone, her thighs pressed only against each other.

A loud groan of frustration echoed in her empty bedroom as Gina opened her eyes. She pressed a hand against her heated forehead.

Another dream. Another faceless lover with eyes that looked

deep into her soul, and filled her heart while he filled her body. Flopping over onto her back in the queen-sized bed, she kicked at the tangled sheets and let the cool air dance across her overheated skin.

She was used to dreams waking her up. When she was a little girl, all her premonitions had come in the form of dreams. But as she grew, so did her skill at manipulating and controlling her gift. Now she could use touch, smell, or even will to bring forth a vision when she needed to. And normally she could block them with equal ease.

She'd had to learn how to block the random vibrations or she wouldn't have been able to live a normal life. But at night, when she sought peace in sleep, sometimes the dreams still came.

The dream with the faceless lover declaring his love had been with her for years, and she wondered if it really was a psychic premonition, or just wishful thinking on her part.

Closing her eyes once more, Gina Devlin trailed a hand over her belly and past the small patch of tight curls. Trying to forget the familiar ache of loneliness in her heart, she concentrated on easing the ache of emptiness between her thighs.

Caleb Mann strode through the heavy glass doors of Fusion Cafe and straight to the service counter. The air conditioning inside the café was a welcome relief from the humid heat of early May in Pearson, British Columbia. Once he had a mug of strong, black coffee in hand, he stepped to the side of the counter and scanned the room.

Fusion Café was on Mason Avenue, the street that ran parallel to Pearson Lake, and the sunlight bounced off the water and brightened the small café. The colorful paintings on the walls and the mismatched furniture gave the café a funky, comfortable feel that was reflected in the diverse clientele. A slick looking businessman stood a couple of feet away, impatiently ordering a fluffy latte from the frowning counter girl. An older lady and a girl who was probably her granddaughter sat with a coloring book in front of them.

None were who he was looking for.

He disregarded the twenty-something male engrossed in a novel nearby and briefly considered the woman by the window. Well-dressed, with long dark hair, she sat ramrod straight watching people come and go. Uncertain, he let his gaze slide away. The he saw her.

Removing his sunglasses, he gave the woman a slow perusal. She'd isolated herself by sitting at a small corner table, head bent over a notepad of some kind. Yet, she still seemed approachable. She was missing that invisible wall that emanated from people when they wanted to be left alone.

She was dressed casually in a short camouflage skirt and a tight black tank top that made it impossible to ignore her pert breasts. If for some unknown reason he hadn't noticed her mouth-watering cleavage, he'd certainly have given the length of tanned flesh exposed by the short skirt a second glance. It had to be her.

Caleb had expected nothing less from his little brother than to set him up with a real looker. What he hadn't expected was his own instant and primal reaction to her. The way his blood heated and his stomach clenched when he looked at her. Or the way her inky black hair, full of vivid red streaks, skimmed across her pale shoulders and made his fingers itch with the urge to brush it aside so he could nibble on her tender flesh.

His reaction surprised him. But for once he didn't try to contain or control it. After all, if she was a friend of his "work hard-play harder" younger brother, chances were she was also a party girl—a bad girl. The total opposite of what he normally looked for in a the fairer sex, and exactly what he needed.

He leaned against the counter and took in the details of the woman. The skimpy clothes and the bare limbs, the bright purple of his fingernails and the silver jewelry, the tattoo on the inside of her wrist. He willed her to lift her head so he could see her face clearly, only to have his breath catch in his throat when she did so.

Flawless skin smoothed over high cheekbones, tiny white

teeth nibbled at a full pink lip, dark eyebrows flared over almond shaped eyes. He couldn't see their color from where he was, but it didn't matter. Her classic beauty and outrageous sex appeal called to him unlike anything, or anyone ever had.

He wanted her, instantly and unequivocally.

Shrugging his suddenly tense shoulders, Caleb pushed off from the counter. He wasn't here to find his soul mate, he reminded himself, just someone to let loose with.

He was tired of everyone ragging on him for being a workaholic. Hell, if he hadn't worked so hard for the past ten years, Gabe wouldn't have been able to go to college. Someone had to pay the bills after their parents died. Plus, his work was satisfying in a way his player of a brother would never understand, so the nagging hadn't bothered him.

Until his last girlfriend dumped him because he was too "old and settled" for her. Then he'd felt a bit of a sting. He was only thirty-three, for God's sake!

Even then her comments hadn't really hurt him, until she'd turned the sting into a downright festering burn by adding that his good looks couldn't compensate for his lack of imagination in the romance department, let alone the bedroom.

Anger, and a twist of uncertainty, burned a hole in his gut. That had been hitting below the belt, literally.

Lack of imagination? He had plenty of imagination. And the wild child girl his little brother had set him up with was going to help him prove it.

Halting next to her table, he pasted a winning smile on his face and opened his mouth.

"Excuse me, Christina?"

When Gina Devlin realized the question was directed at her, she huffed out a grateful breath and tossed aside her charcoal pencil. Normally she didn't welcome interruptions when she was working, but her muse had deserted her, taking any semblance of artistic talent along with it.

Eager for a distraction, she leaned back in her chair, looked over the wall of muscle standing next to her corner table with a big grin on his gorgeous face. Gina immediately felt her skin begin to itch from the inside out. He was her favorite type of distraction . . . male.

His buttoned-up shirt and pressed jeans did nothing to detract from the wide shoulders and slim hips they covered. However, in her mind they labeled him a stickler for the rules, and totally not her type. Only a real stick-in-the-mud would iron his jeans.

The fact that he wasn't her type didn't stop her eyes from continuing to skim appreciatively over his trim hips, the impressive package between them, and down his muscled thighs before rising back up to meet his steady gaze.

A gaze that was vaguely familiar. Shaking off that thought, she realized that he'd called her Christina.

The little devil inside her strained at the leash she'd kept him on for the last six months. Poking her with his pointy tail he screamed, "Do it! Do it!"

Before she could think twice, her lips parted and the words tumbled out. "I prefer Tina."

2

"I'm Caleb. Gabe's brother." The stranger held out a large hand to her.

His voice was smooth and deep, making shivers skip down her spine. She leaned forward, slipping her hand into his. Long fingers wrapped gently around her hand, the heat of him soaked through her skin, inching its way up her arm. Her palm tingled and images of open mouths, sweaty bodies, and tangled sheets filled her mind.

Whoa!

She pulled her hand away in surprise. To cover up her sudden disquiet over the vision, she waved the hand blithely at the empty seat across from her. "Have a seat, Caleb."

What was she thinking? Or better yet, what was she doing? She had a deadline; she didn't have any time to waste on a man, no matter how good-looking he was. Of course, it was rare for her to get a psychic flash just from shaking hands with stranger. Rarer still for the vision to be one that made her body flush with heat.

Gina eyed Caleb from under he lashes as he settled into the

chair across from her. He set his coffee mug gently on the table and settled his large body into the tiny iron chair. This guy was here to meet someone else. Despite his good looks and awesome body, he wasn't exactly her type. Maybe she should've reined in the little devil, and let him move on.

Then again, there was no such thing as a coincidence. Right? Therefore, he was meant to meet her. She'd been struggling with her new collection of sketches anyway. Her muse had given up on her and run away to have some fun. Maybe she should do the same. She couldn't remember the last time she forgot about everything but having a good time. And if the vision of hot sweaty bodies rolling around together she'd had when they shook hands was any indication, this man could show her a *really* good time.

With a mental shrug she smiled flirtatiously at her tablemate. The hunk smiled back, his blue eyes twinkling playfully. There was a brief silence while they openly checked one another out. She shifted in her seat and crossed her legs, getting comfortable. When she saw the way his eyes followed her movements she fought back a wicked grin. Even dressed as she was, in causal just-off-work clothes, she knew she looked good. Then they both spoke at once.

"How do you . . ."

"So what do you . . ."

They laughed together and the tension eased. Caleb settled back in his chair, spreading his hands wide. "Ladies first," he said with a crooked smile.

Relishing the jump in her pulse at his smile, she leaned forward, giving him a clear view of her cleavage, and arched an eyebrow at him. "I was just going to ask what you liked to do for fun?"

Heat warmed his gaze, but Gina was pleased to see that

while he glanced at the offered view, he didn't stare crudely. Instead he locked eyes with her and showed off perfectly white teeth in a sardonic smile before he answered softly.

"I haven't made much time for fun lately. In fact, just the other day I was accused of being old and stodgy."

"You?" She chuckled softly. "You look like you might be a little uptight. But definitely not old, and well . . . stodgy we can fix."

He looked at little taken aback by her bluntness, but he didn't run away. "That's good to hear. I will admit I've let business, and various responsibilities take over a large chunk of my life in the past. My construction company is doing well now, and I've decided it's time for a change. Time to stop making work the focus of my life." He stared at her with earnest blue eyes. "That's why I agreed to this blind date. It's time to try new things and remember how to have a good time."

Gina understood the demands of starting and running one's own business. Her artwork was a business for her, a part-time one, but still a business. But she also knew that sometimes a body just had to ignore business, and concentrate on pleasure.

She scanned the room and didn't notice a single woman alone anywhere. Deciding that Caleb's date had either missed him, or pulled a no-show, she locked eyes with him and kicked things up a notch. "Do you have anything specific in mind for fun, or are you open to pretty much anything?"

The flickering flames in his eyes burned hotter at her challenge and his smile turned wolfish. "I'm ready for anything."

She fought the urge to crow in delight. He wasn't as uptight as she'd thought. So what if he put his business before pleasure? A sense of responsibility isn't really a *bad* thing in a man. And this man definitely had bad-boy potential. She could sense it.

Adrenaline pumped through her veins and her inner bad girl roared to life, ready and willing to face all challengers. She felt alive. Fully energized for the first time in longer than she could remember.

She grinned at Caleb. It was time to play.

"I think I can help you out," she said with cocky confidence. Giving her sketch pad one last look, she shoved it into her canvas tote bag and gestured towards the door. "Let's go somewhere with a bit more action and see what happens."

She'd surprised him.

Not many people could do that.

Caleb wasn't sure what he expected when they left the coffee shop. But this wasn't it. When he watched her swing a slender leg over the seat of a sexy little crotch-rocket of a motorcycle, leaving her thighs almost completely bare, it had never entered his mind that they would end up in a gay bar.

Not that he minded. He didn't judge people by their sexual preference. It just wasn't somewhere he would've thought to take a woman he hoped to get intimate with.

A quick glance around the dark room made him reconsider. It was early and the bar wasn't full, but it was busy enough. Yet no one bothered them, or even gave second look.

There were same sex couples, male and female, lounging on various sofas surrounding the room's perimeter, a small group of young men stationed in the front of the bar, and a male couple on the dance floor swaying back and forth in each other's arms.

When he really thought about it, it was the perfect place to get to know someone. Everyone there was intent on doing his or her own thing. No one would bother them.

With his back to the wall, he had a clear view of the room, and of Tina's antics. They'd been playing pool for almost two hours, and despite the fact that he'd been in a constant state of semi-arousal through it all, he'd learned some pretty interesting things about her.

In fact, she fascinated him.

"You mean to tell me that you work at the coffee shop, making sandwiches and lattes for people every day, when you could easily support yourself with your illustrations?" It didn't make sense to him. He could tell by the tone of her voice when she talked about her art that she loved painting, so why would she want to work in a café when she could make a living doing what she loved?

Her lush breast brushed against his arm as she reached past him for the cube of chalk on the edge of the table, heating his blood up another degree. He wondered if she was deliberately trying to drive him insane with lust, but the innocent look on her face as she chalked her stick made it hard to tell.

"My artwork pays nicely, but if I devoted myself to it entirely, I could easily become a hermit. Working in the café lets me deal with real people without getting too close to them."

"You don't like getting close to people?" He watched as she strolled to the end of the table and lined up her shot.

She bent over at the waist and he got an eyeful of plum womanly flesh cupped lovingly in fire engine red satin. "I love getting close to the right people," she said in a husky voice.

Swallowing hard, he dragged his gaze from her cleavage to her delicate face. The devilish glint in her dark eyes left no doubt in his mind that he could be one of the lucky ones. One of the people she might get *real* close to.

Unsure of how to handle such blatant flirting, he focused his attention on the pool table, and mentioned his love for his own work. Flirting was one of those things he just never got the hang of. It was too much of an iffy thing, a grey area that was always open to interpretation. He preferred to deal in things that were solid . . . black and white only.

Tina's lips twitched up on one side but she didn't say anything, she just let the conversation move on, and continued to kick his ass at pool.

It wasn't surprising she was winning. Watching her bend and stretch over the green felt that somehow reminded him of his bed was much more distracting than playing with one of the guys. Yet he felt like he was getting to know her better than he ever could while sitting across from her at a dinner table.

"So you enjoy working with your hands then?" she asked in reference to his comment about preferring to work with his crew instead of just supervising. The comment itself wasn't sexual. But to his fogged brain, everything she said and did had sexual connotations. He was having a hard time being the gentleman he prided himself on being.

Thoughts of getting to know her better in any but the physical sense disappeared as she stretched a bit further to line up another shot and her skirt rose another inch. Half an inch more and he'd know what color her panties were. Or if she even had any on. Which he didn't think she did.

In his mind's-eye, he undid the zipper of his jeans and stepped up behind her. Lifting her skirt that final bit, he'd thrust into her from behind. She would grip the edge of the pool table and push back against him. No one would even notice if they were quiet.

Ungluing his gaze from her legs, and the temptation they represented, he shifted his stance. He glanced around the bar in an effort to distract his mind and keep his zipper from splitting.

What's going on? He'd never had a problem with control before. Somehow, Tina's body called out to the caveman in him, and his baser urges were fast erasing his common sense. Along with his ability to hold a decent conversation. What had they been talking about?

He watched the cue stick slide through her purple tipped

fingers and bit back a groan. Hands, she'd asked if he liked to work with his hands.

"Yeah," he tried desperately to get his mind back on topic. "There are few things as satisfying as looking at a completed project, and knowing you built it with your own two hands."

He'd never fantasized about sex in public before. Hell, he'd never even had sex anywhere other than a bed. He and his brother had been raised to treat women like ladies. He wined and dined them if he wanted to get to know them. And unlike his brother Gabriel, he always got to know them before going to bed with them.

A lightning bolt of realization hit him between the eyes and he groaned softly. His head fell back, thunking against the wall, and his eyes slid closed in misery.

He *was* a boring lover.

"What's wrong?"

Her small hand burned through his shirt, leaving an imprint right over his pounding heart. He straightened up, praying that she couldn't read his mind, and looked down at the sex kitten standing in front of him. A party girl his wild younger brother had set him up with. Did he really think he could please her?

She cocked her head to the side and studied him for a minute. A flame flickered to life in the depths of her dark eyes. Her full lips slowly tilted into a naughty smile. Without another word, she stepped closer, brushing her body against his, her breath dancing across his chin.

Regret fought with desire as her hand slid around his neck and she pulled his head closer to hers. She didn't know what sort of a letdown she was setting herself up for. Her tongue darted out, and he watched it teasingly wet her lips before they pressed softly against his.

All thoughts ceased. She leaned her body against him fully and nudged his lips apart with the tip of her tongue. Determined to shake his insecurities, he dove into the kiss. Thrusting his hands into her silky hair, he gave into his lust.

He needed this. Needed to feel the hot eagerness of a woman against him, sighing in pleasure and wanting only him. Tongues tangled and heat burned through veins.

A deep groan formed in his chest and he tore his mouth away from her and she boldly rubbed against him. Burying his face in the curve of her neck, he nipped at the soft skin there. He tasted her flavor and let his hands roam greedily over her curves.

He spread his thighs, pulled her tight against him and felt her press against the ache of his confined cock. Unfortunately, the eager gyrating of her hips only encouraged him to lose control.

The abundance of her rounded ass filled his hands while he held her still and thrust against her soft warmth. Her sharp teeth nipped his earlobe just before he trailed his lips across her collarbone and down to the swell of her breasts. He couldn't get enough.

Closer, he needed to get closer. Her clothing was in the way. He inhaled deeply of her sweet scent before nudging aside the hem of her skirt in search of bare flesh.

A distinct pain bit into his skull and his head was pulled back sharply.

"Down boy, we don't want to get arrested now, do we?"

Tina's husky voice brought him back to reality with a shudder. She was breathing as heavily as he was, and her fingers stroked soothingly though the hair at the nape of his neck. The hair she'd pulled to get him to back off.

A groan escaped from him and he closed his eyes against the truth of it. If she hadn't stopped him he didn't think he would've stopped. How was he ever going to make her pant and beg and call out his name, if he couldn't even control himself in public?